T0312342

# Clean

# Clean

## Alia Trabucco Zerán

*Translated from the Spanish*
*by Sophie Hughes*

4th ESTATE • *London*

4th Estate
An imprint of HarperCollins*Publishers*
1 London Bridge Street
London SE1 9GF

www.4thestate.co.uk

HarperCollins*Publishers*
Macken House, 39/40 Mayor Street Upper
Dublin 1, D01 C9W8, Ireland

First published as *Limpia* by Lumen Press in 2022
First published in Great Britain in 2024 by 4th Estate

1



A catalogue record for this book is available from the British Library

ISBN 978-0-00-860793-7 (hardback)
ISBN 978-0-00-860794-4 (trade paperback)



Set in Stempel Garamond
Printed and bound in the UK using 100% renewable electricity at CPI Group (UK) Ltd

'... it's a question of which will clean up the other.'

Albert Camus, *The Fall*
translated by Justin O'Brien

My name is Estela. Can you hear me? I said: Es-te-la-Gar-cí-a.

I don't know if you're recording this or taking notes or if there's anyone even over there. But if you can hear me, if you are there, then I want to propose a deal: I'm going to tell you a story, and when I get to the end, when I stop talking, you're going to let me out of here.

Hello? Nothing?

I'll take your silence as a yes.

This story has several beginnings. I'd go as far as to say it's made up of beginnings. But tell me: what defines a beginning? Explain to me, for example, whether night comes before day or day before night. Whether we wake because we went to sleep or sleep because we woke up. Or better, to keep things simple, just tell me where a tree begins: in the seed or the fruit around it? Or perhaps it's in the branch that grew the flower that turned into the fruit? Or in the flower itself? Are you with me? Nothing is ever as simple as it seems.

The same goes for causes, they're just as unclear as beginnings. The cause of my thirst or hunger, for example. The cause of my current confinement. One cause sets off another, one card brings down the next. The only given is the ending: nothing's left standing. And the end of this story – are you sure you want to know? – is this:

The girl dies.

Hello? No reaction at all?

Let me say it again in case a fly buzzed in your ear. Or perhaps you were put off by a sharper, shriller thought than my voice:

The girl dies. Did you hear this time? The girl dies and she's still dead, no matter where I begin.

But death isn't so simple either, that much I'm sure we can agree on. Deaths are a little like shadows: they differ in length and breadth from person to person, creature to creature, tree to tree. No two shadows on the earth's surface are the same, and no two deaths are either. Every lamb, every spider, every chincol dies in its own way.

Take rabbits, for example ... stay with me, it's important. Have you ever held a rabbit in your hands? It's like cradling a grenade, a velvety time bomb. Tick tock, tick tock, tick tock, tick tock. Rabbits are the only creatures on earth that are regularly scared to death. If a rabbit picks up a fox's scent or senses a snake nearby, its heart starts racing and its pupils dilate. The adrenaline is like a hammer to the heart and the rabbit dies before the predator can sink its fangs into its neck. It's fear that kills it, you see? Sheer anticipation. All within a fraction of a second the rabbit realises it's going to die, glimpses how and when. And this conviction, this foretelling of its imminent end, is its death sentence.

It doesn't happen like that for house sparrows or cats, lizards or bees. And what to say about plants: the death of a willow or hydrangea, an ulmo or winter's bark. Or the end of a fig tree, with its cement-like solid grey trunk. It would take a very powerful cause to kill a hardy fig. A deadly fungus slowly spreading through its branches until eventually, after decades, the tree's roots rot away. Or a handsaw hacking it down and chopping its trunk into firewood.

Every species, every living creature on the planet must find its own proper cause of death. A sufficient reason. One capable of crushing a life. And life, as you know, clings to some bodies. It fights back, thriving and dogged, and won't be easily prised away. For that you need the appropriate tool: soap for a stain, tweezers for a thorn. Can you hear me over there? Are you paying attention? A fish can't drown underwater. And a fishhook will barely scratch the roof of a whale's mouth. But you can't overdo death either; you can't die in excess.

I am getting to the point, don't worry. This is the edge of the story, and it's right to hang back at the edge before diving in. It's right that you understand how I came to be locked up, the events that led me here. And for you to glimpse, piece by piece, the girl's cause of death.

I've killed before, it's true. I promise not to lie to you. I've killed flies and moths, chickens, worms, a fern and a rose bush. And a long time ago, out of pity, I killed a wounded piglet. On that occasion I did feel sad, but I killed it because it was dying. It was dying a slow and painful death, so I got there first.

But those deaths don't interest you. They're not what you want to hear about. Don't worry, I'll get to the point, to the longed-for cause of death. A fistful of pills, a plane crash, a noose slung around a neck – some people survive against all the odds. For them the task of dying isn't so easy. Men who need to be mown down by a lorry or have a bullet pumped into their chest. Women who jump from the sixth floor because the fifth wouldn't cut it. For others, though, all it takes is a case of pneumonia, or a chill, or a fruit stone lodged in their throat. And for a very rare few, like the girl, just an idea will do. A lethal idea, born in a moment of weakness. I'll tell you about that idea, about when it came to her. Now stop what you're doing and listen to me.

The advertisement read like this:

Housemaid wanted, presentable, full time.

They gave a telephone number, which led to an address, and it was to that address that I set off, in a white blouse and this black skirt I'm wearing now.

They met me at the door, the pair of them. I'm talking about the señor and señora, the houseowners, the employers, the relatives of the deceased. You'll come up with your own name for them, I'm sure. She opened the door, pregnant, and as she went to shake my hand, she looked me up and down, taking in my hair, my clothes, my still-white plimsolls. A thorough inspection, as if that would reveal to her some important detail about me. He, on the other hand, didn't so much as look at me. He was texting on his phone and, without even glancing up, pointed at the kitchen door.

I can't reproduce their questions for me word for word, but I do remember one quite curious detail. He was clean-shaven and there was a wisp of bright shaving foam just below his right sideburn.

Hello? What is it? The maid can't use the word 'wisp'?

I thought I heard laughter, and not the friendly kind, on the other side of this wall.

As I was saying, that mark on his skin unsettled me. It was like a tiny piece of skin had been torn from his face, but underneath, instead of flesh and blood, was something white, artificial. The señora noticed that I couldn't stop staring at him, and when at last she spotted the foam, she licked her thumb and wiped it away with her spit.

You'll be wondering: How is any of this relevant? It isn't, that's the answer. Apart from that I clearly recall his reaction, the way he removed his wife's hand, reproaching her for that display of intimacy in front of a perfect stranger. A few weeks later, I was making the master bed when the señor suddenly appeared out of the bathroom. I thought he'd already left for work, but there he was standing stark naked in front of me. He didn't jump, he wasn't even flustered. Without batting an eyelid, he went to get a pair of underpants, returned to the bathroom and shut the door behind him. Perhaps you can explain what happened between our first meeting and that one.

They needed someone to start as soon as possible.

The señor said:

Ideally on Monday.

The señora:

Ideally today.

Stuck to the fridge was a piece of paper listing all the jobs I'd be expected to carry out. This way they wouldn't have to ask their eventual maid outright if she could read, if she was capable of writing the shopping list or taking down phone messages. I went over, read the list, took the piece of paper and put it in my pocket. Neat, assertive, a sufficiently well-educated maid.

I can start on Monday, I said.

They accepted right away, without even requesting references. I later learned that everything happened against the clock in that house, although what the great hurry was I never understood. Haste makes waste. That's what my mama used to say whenever I flew out of the house late for school and cut across the vegetable garden. You'll never beat time at its own game, she'd warn me. That race is fixed from the day we're born. But I've been sidetracked ... I was telling you about how there were never enough hours in that family's day, and how few days were left before the birth of their first daughter.

I know what you're going to ask me, and the answer is no. I didn't have any experience with children, and I didn't lie to them about it. My mama had told me on the phone: Don't lie to them, Lita. You never lie on the first day. So I told them, quite openly:

I don't have any children. I don't have any nieces or nephews. I've never changed a nappy.

But they'd made their decision. The señora had liked my white blouse, my long, neat plait, my clean, straight teeth, and the fact that at no point had I dared to hold her gaze.

As soon as the questions were over, they showed me the rest of the house:

This is the broom cupboard, Estela.

The rubber gloves, the mop.

Here's the first aid kit.

Sponges, bleach, detergent, fresh linen.

Here's the ironing board, the laundry basket.

The soap, the washing machine, the sewing basket, the tools.

Nothing should be left to go mouldy, Estela.

Don't let any food go out of date.

Deep clean on Mondays.

Water the garden in the evening.

And never, under any circumstance, open the door to anyone.

I don't remember much else from that day apart from one thought, which has stayed with me. As I made my way down the hallway, running my eyes over the bathrooms, looking into each of the rooms, as I took in the living room, the dining room, the outdoor terrace and the swimming pool, I thought, very clearly: this is a real house, with nails hammered into the walls and picture frames hanging from those nails. And that thought, I don't know why, brought on a pain between my eyes. Like a flame burning me in this space right here.

They didn't show me the back room on the day of the interview. I'm talking about the room they called 'your room' and that I'll call 'the back room'. I discovered it on the following Monday, my first day of work. The señora opened the front door to me, her face pale and clammy.

Make yourself at home, she said, and she disappeared off to take a rest.

I entered the kitchen, alone, and was surprised not to have noticed the unusual door in there before. It blended in with the stone wall tiles, like the entrance to a hidden vault. I walked over and slid it open. You'd already guessed it was a sliding door? To maximise space. To prevent it from banging against the bed. It didn't push open like a normal door, so I slid it to the left and took my first step inside that room.

Make a note of what was inside in case it's somehow important: a single bed, a small nightstand, a bedside lamp, a chest of drawers and an old TV set. Inside the dresser were six uniforms: Monday, Tuesday, Wednesday, Thursday, Friday, Saturday. Sunday was my free day. There were no pictures on the walls, no ornaments, just a small window and a shower room, home to an old vanity, and a few damp patches that looked like mouths laughing their heads off.

I closed the door behind me and stood there, my lips suddenly dry. I could feel my legs start to go so I sat down on the edge of the bed. Then another feeling came over me … how can I describe it. I felt like I hadn't really entered that room, but rather was standing outside of it watching the woman I was to become from that moment: her fingers interlaced on her lap, her eyes sore, her lips parched and her breathing heavy. I noticed then the textured, frosted glass on the sliding door. I'm guessing the señor has already used one of his favourite words on you: 'fluted'. A fluted, frosted glass door connecting the bedroom to the kitchen. And that's where I lived for seven years, although never, not once, did I refer to it as 'my room'. Write that down in your notes, go on, don't be shy: 'Categorically refuses to refer to the bedroom as "her room".' And then add in the margin: 'denial', 'resentment', 'possible motive'.

Shortly afterwards I heard someone enter the kitchen and wait for me outside … or inside. I don't know. Maybe that bedroom was actually outside, meaning the kitchen was inside. Certain details are unclear, at least to me: inside, outside; present, past; before, after.

The señora audibly cleared her throat. I gulped and said: I'm coming.

Or maybe no one cleared their throat and I didn't say a word, and that woman, the one I would become for the next seven years, simply got undressed and pulled her uniform over her head. It felt very close-fitting at the neck, too tight for me, but when I went to undo the top button I realised there was no buttonhole. A decorative button at the housemaid's throat. The other five uniforms all had the same fake fastening.

It's odd that I remember this detail and yet haven't the faintest idea what I did for the rest of the day. I have no idea if I cooked. I don't know if I cleaned. I don't know if I watered the garden or did the ironing. The one thing I do remember about those first two weeks is our endless game of cat and mouse. If I entered the living room, the señora would quietly slip into the dining room. If I entered the dining room, she would disappear off to the bathroom. If I wanted to clean the bathroom, she would shut herself away in her office. I didn't know what to do, where to put myself. Her bump made it hard for her to get around, but she would rather make an escape than be left on her own and in silence with a stranger. Because that's what I was, a stranger. I don't know when exactly I stopped being one. Maybe when she started asking me to handwash her knickers, or saying things like: Estelita, the girl's just been sick. Splash some bleach on the floor, please.

But ask her when my birthday is. Ask her how old I am.

That first week they didn't even know what to call me. They kept going to say the name of the woman who'd worked in the house before. The one who used to scrub the bottom of their toilet bowl and take out their bins every

Tuesday and Friday. The woman who made them Russian salad and saw them lying in bed. They never told me what she was called, but I can take a good guess because they were both incapable of getting my name out correctly.

Mmmestela, they'd say.

To this day I still think about what the name of that woman who came before me might have been: María, Marisela, Mariela, Mónica. What I do know for sure is the first initial; it took months to disappear.

For my part, I always referred to my boss as 'the señora'. The señora isn't at home. Will the señora be wanting lunch? What time will the señora be back? But her name is Mara, Doña Mara López. I'm sure when you called her in and she looked at you with that expression of hers – like she'd just noticed a stain, or a mistake – you must have said: 'Señora Mara, please, take a seat. Would you like a glass of water? Some tea? Sugar or sweetener?', wondering all the while, as I did, who on earth has a name like Mara. It's like calling yourself Jula or Veronca. Like living with a part missing.

There was something about her. A sort of, let me think ... detachment. But, actually, that's not the right word. Contempt, that's it. As if everyone bored her, or as if she were repulsed by any kind of complicity. At least that was the front she put up. The mask she donned each morning. Underneath it she'd go red with rage whenever her husband came home late from work, or her daughter spat her already chewed food back onto the plate. One of her eyelids, the left one, would visibly twitch, as if a little piece of her own face wanted to break free and never return.

But there I go, digressing again. It must be the lack of practice. The señora's face isn't relevant. I should talk to you about him.

I referred to him as, you guessed it, 'the señor', although sometimes I called him 'your dad'. Where's your dad? Is your dad home yet? But his name is Cristóbal. Don Juan Cristóbal Jensen. A gruff sort of man with a prematurely receding hairline and blue eyes the colour of a pilot light. Every morning, before leaving for work, he'd mutter to himself exactly the same line: Back to the grind. It was either some kind of a ritual, or he really did detest it. His job, I mean. Don't act surprised. He hated his colleagues, the nurses, every one of his patients. You must have seen him in his crisply pressed shirt, his brightly polished shoes, waiting for someone to thank him for saving their life. Or maybe he wore his white coat when he was here, to make sure you called him 'Doctor'. Now, that he really did love, when someone called him 'Doctor Jensen'. But write this down on your notepads: being a doctor means nothing. Not when your only daughter dies. Not when you can't save her.

We seldom spoke, he and I. All I had to do was serve him his food promptly and keep his shirts clean and ironed. I can't think how else to describe him. Maybe you can help. How would you define a person who doesn't smoke, who barely drinks, who weighs up every word before speaking to avoid causing a scene, because a scene would only waste his time. A man obsessed with time:

We'll eat in an hour, Estela.

Heat up the food in fifteen minutes.

I'm running ten minutes late for clinic.

I've got two minutes for breakfast.

I'll be there in one minute, open the front gate.

I'm going to count down from three.

Two.

One.

A perpetual countdown.

The girl was born on 15 March, a week after I arrived. The sound of the señora's screams absolutely horrified me, each one followed by a single instruction: breathe.

It was five in the morning and I'd been asleep, although who knows really. Sometimes I question whether I ever got a second's sleep in that room. In any case the screaming startled me, so I got up and went into the hallway. The señora was holding her belly. The señor had his arm around her waist and was trying to convince her to walk to the car. One step, a scream. Two steps, another scream. She was going on as if there were no limit to the number of screams a person can let out in their lifetime; as if each one weren't worth a million words.

They returned several days later. I was expecting them much sooner, but there had been complications during the labour which nobody told me about. What for? Why should the housemaid need to know? It was strange, that wait. They weren't in the house but neither had they fully left it. I remember spending hour after hour sitting at the kitchen table with my hands resting on the tabletop and my gaze fixed on the TV screen above the fridge: historic drought across the country, roadblocks in Araucanía, washing machine flash sale. That's how I spent my days: poised between calamities and commercials. I suppose I could have made the most of that time to have a dip in the pool, to chat on the phone all afternoon, to polish off the leftover whiskey and try on the señora's jewellery. That's what you were thinking, right? Don't make me laugh.

Then, one morning, I heard the car pull up and the keys in the front door latch. I expected to hear crying, but the child didn't make a sound. She didn't cry when she was born, did you know that? The señor joked about that silence every time his daughter had a meltdown. Every time it proved impossible to bring their tetchy little girl down from one of her tantrums, he and his wife would recall how their daughter had been completely mute for the first few days of her life. As if she had no need of anything. As if she'd been born satisfied.

The señora was holding that bundle in her arms and wearing a stiff, forced smile, almost like a grimace of terror. I noticed that the effort of walking from the car had left her exhausted. Her lips were chapped and her face was haggard and grey, covered in a film of sweat that would take weeks to disappear. Open the windows, Estela, the doors, all the doors, let some air in the house, please. That's what she said, please, as if it were a favour that she'd one day return.

She took a few short steps, stopped in the doorway and let out a heavy sigh. I think that was the only time I ever felt sorry for the señora. I felt bad seeing her that tired, so I held out my arms and took her daughter. That's people for you, isn't it? That's what my mama used to say whenever she left a saucer of milk out for the stray dogs in Plaza de Ancud. That's people for you, she'd say, again and again, whenever she agreed to take in an abandoned cat or carry some old fellow's shopping from the market to his house. That's what people are like, that's what people are like. But it's not true. It's not what people are like. Underline that when you write this down.

Taking the girl in my arms I was surprised by how little she weighed: so slight, so fragile it made you want to cry. Her puffy eyes and round face were like those of any other newborn. And she had that same smell and the shell-shocked, unfocused look babies have when they first open their eyes. She was smaller than I'd imagined, but then, what did I know. In no time she would start to grow, her nails would grow and I'd have to cut them thousands of times over the course of a long and vigorous life, which is how a life should be.

With the girl now placed in my arms the señora said she needed to rest and that I must watch her. She didn't use her name, you know. She just said 'her'. Watch her, Estela. Get her to sleep, please. Maybe that's why to me she was always just 'the girl', even though her real name was Julia. But you must know that already too.

I carried her to the bedroom at the far end of the hallway. They'd decorated it with daisy-patterned wallpaper, a wooden crib and a mobile with zebras and suns that never stopped turning. I put her down on the wicker changing table and started to undress her. First her thick fleece quilt, then the cotton blanket, then her onesie, which was too big for her. Having undressed her down to her nappy I was able to see the rest of her body. Blotchy with yellow patches and the brownish black cord stump hanging from her belly button. She squirmed at the contact with the cold, but she didn't cry. Out of her gummy mouth came only air, nothing else. But it would fill up with words, that mouth: give, want, come, no.

I unstuck the tabs on her nappy and a vinegary smell flooded the room. I thought newborn babies weren't supposed to smell, but what did I know. Shit is shit, no matter where it's come from, my mama used to say as she cleaned out the pig's pen or the cesspit out on the land, and I suppose she was right.

With some wet wipes I cleaned the girl until she was spotless. Next I put her in a fresh nappy and a smaller onesie, then, finally, I slid a pair of tiny white mittens on her hands. I'd heard that babies often scratch their faces after birth. What sort of instinct is that: to come out into the world and claw at your own face.

I picked her up and only then did she half open her eyes. They were grey in colour, lost, incapable of seeing the edges of things. In that moment I thought: that must be true silence, when everything around you becomes blurred. And I rocked her to pull myself out of the silence that was already threatening to engulf me. Luckily, the girl fell straight to sleep. Or maybe she stayed awake but just closed her eyes, I don't know. I laid her down gently in her cot and watched her settle into that space. I'd never looked after a child before, let alone a newborn. I told the señora that when she hired me, but she just assumed her maid would know how to use the washing machine, the iron, a needle and thread. And, of course, how to look after her child. Her Julia, who really was sleeping now, letting out high-pitched, forlorn little whimpers.

I don't know how much time went by. How long I spent guarding that little girl's sleep: ten minutes, seven years, the rest of my life. I stood there, frozen, leaning over the edge of her cot, unable to take my eyes off that chest as it rose and fell, incapable of telling affection from despair.

One morning, and this was on one of my first days, after showering and putting on my uniform, I went into the kitchen to find a note on the fridge door. I was surprised the señora hadn't told me she'd be taking the baby out so early. It's a test, I thought. She wanted to know whether the new maid, when left to her own devices in the house, would take the first opportunity to call up her aunts, her female cousins and her countless nieces for a gossip instead of working.

I checked the phone wasn't off the hook and returned to the note:

Washing-up liquid

Nappies

Low-fat yogurt

Wholemeal bread

Words and a banknote, which I pushed down deep into my pocket. Literate, trustworthy, presentable.

The sound of the phone ringing made me jump. It would be the señora, who else? Of course it was her, but I didn't know what to do. Should I answer to show her that the new maid was paying attention? Or not answer, letting the dial tone slowly drive the señora mad but at the same time showing her, at the other end, something even more valuable: that the line was unengaged and her efficient maid already on her way to the supermarket.

I didn't pick up.

Outside, the heat had decimated the laurels, now limp from too much sun. I left the house as I was, dressed in my uniform and plimsolls, and ahead of me I spotted a woman walking on the other side of the road. She was dressed exactly like me: the same grey and black checked uniform, the same fake button, the same plait and plimsolls. She was walking very slowly with an elderly lady who had pearl earrings, a handbag hanging from her shoulder, and dyed, coiffured hair. I take that back … it wasn't quite like that. The woman wasn't walking *with* that elderly lady. She was supporting her with great difficulty, shuffling along awkwardly with her back bent over from the weight. The woman in the uniform noticed me, we glanced at one another and both stopped where we were. Her face was my face, that's what I thought, and a shudder ran through me. If I let go, if I suddenly turned and bolted, the old lady at that other woman's side would fall flat on her face.

I walked off very quickly in the opposite direction. I didn't know which way it was to the supermarket but the mere thought of walking in step with that other woman was unbearable. I passed some private residential streets and gated houses. It was late summer and some of the trees had begun to lose their first leaves, but the ground was impeccable, recently swept. The pavement had no cracks, the street was lined with trees and there wasn't a bus to be seen. Like a film set, that's what I thought, and I picked up my pace.

I think it was my excessively calm surroundings that made me notice someone was following me. A shadow, a rustle; it must have been that woman, the one I was going to become in a few years, treading on the heels of my own plimsolls, whispering some secret in my own ear. I felt my heart beating faster and my hands go cold and clammy. I was convinced I was going to faint, smash my head against the hard ground. I'd wake up in a hospital. The señora would fire me for being feeble, for being weak. I'd have to go back to the island and admit that my mama had been right: it had been a big mistake, I never should have moved to Santiago. Then I said to myself: Estela, enough. And I turned back and carried on walking.

House after house, electric fence after electric fence, and not a soul on the pavement. We were in the middle of a drought, as you know, but the grass, the front gardens, the flowerbeds were all still green. A harmonious, peaceful neighbourhood. A miniature city within a city. Stopping to catch my breath, I wiped my hands on my uniform and saw, up ahead on the corner, a petrol station and, at long last, the damn supermarket.

I crossed the street and cut across the petrol station forecourt, right past the pump. I don't know why I did it. Why did I want to take a shortcut, save time, get there quicker? The guy attending the pump stared at me for far longer than you're meant to look at another person. Either he didn't mind making me uncomfortable, or that was precisely his intention. But then again, who goes around in public in her maid's uniform with such a panic-stricken look on her face? I watched him out of the corner of my eye. He was young, skinny, with a fern tattooed on his arm and a huge brown dog at his feet. He didn't take his eyes off me until I was inside the supermarket. As if that woman – as if I, that is – were a genuine apparition.

The special offers announcement snapped me out of it and I took the shopping list from my pocket:

Washing-up liquid
Nappies
Low-fat yogurt
Wholemeal bread

I crossed out each item like you're probably crossing out certain words of mine. The ones you consider to be inappropriate or implausible; the ones you deem not to fit. I paid, put away the receipt, counted the change and went back outside. Now listen carefully, my friends, I'm talking to you. Yes, you lot over there, waiting for a confession. What's the matter? I thought I heard someone protesting on the other side of the door. Does it bother you, my calling you 'friends'? Too overfamiliar? What would you like me to call you? Your Excellency, Your Honour? Esteemed Ladies and Gentleman?

On more than one occasion I've wondered who you are, and whether, if I moved closer to the glass, I might catch a glimpse of your faces. But no matter how close I get, I only ever see my own reflection looking back at me. So I study my eyes, my mouth, the first wrinkles on my forehead, and I ask myself if tiredness is a phase and if one day, in the future, I'll get my old face back.

I know I'm going off track again, but be patient with me. When I stepped outside of the supermarket I felt the sun's heat flood my whole body, and then *that thing* happened for the first time. I looked up, gazed around me, and I didn't know where I was. It's not a figure of speech. I never knew how to be poetic. I ran my eyes over the road, over the leaves quivering on the branches of the soapbarks, over the name written on the sign above the petrol pump. But the more I looked at the reality around me, the less able I felt to decipher how I'd got there, to that street, that neighbourhood, that city, that job. I couldn't tell the soil from the asphalt, a bicycle from an animal, one leg from another, that other maid from me. The very idea of an animal, of paved earth, of the maid walking under the hot sun in her uniform was suddenly far removed, strange. Having somehow folded inside out, I'd ended up there and now I could no longer leave.

I stood, dazzled by the light, frozen with fear, searching desperately for something to bring me back to my own body. I slapped my cheeks several times and rubbed my eyes with my fists. Then I spotted that dog again: brown, straggly, a wild look in its eye. The dog, the fern tattoo on the young man's arm, the spotless street, that woman who I would one day become, taking her elderly employer for a walk. I remembered the way back and hurried off in the direction of the house.

I hadn't even set foot through the front door when I heard the phone ring.

Señora, that's what I said, not even waiting for her to speak.

She wanted to know how I'd known who was calling. I didn't reply. Why bother? My hands were still shaking and I wanted to sit down for a minute, but instead I'd have to go straight back to the supermarket. The señora had forgotten to add olive oil and soap to the list.

Buenos días, Estela.

Buenos días, Señor.

Buenas noches, Estela.

Buenas noches, Señora.

Open your eyes, get out of bed, jump in the shower. Put on your uniform, plait your hair, head into the kitchen. Boil some water, make tea, eat some bread and butter. Prepare their breakfast, take it to them in bed, receive instructions for the day.

Once they've left for work, enter the master bedroom. Pick the pyjamas off the floor, open the windows, listen to the parrots' frenzied squawks in the pine tree. Gather the bedspread and blankets and roll them up at the foot of the mattress. Then strip the sheets, shake them out hard and watch the fabric inflate like a big parachute.

I made the master bed every day I worked in that house. That makes more than two thousand mornings: I hadn't added them up until now. Two thousand plus times that I looked at those creases on the bottom sheet. Lint balls at the foot end from where the señor and the señora kicked and jerked in the night. I always found that strange. Strange that they should thrash about enough to wear down their socks like that. I've always slept like a mummy, ever since I was a girl, maybe because I mostly shared the bed with my mama. In the summer we'd stick to our own sides of the mattress, but in the winter I was afraid that the wind would rip off the zinc roof sheets or that the house would be pulled right down to the beach in a mudslide or that an enormous old eucalyptus would fall on top of us. So I would twist and turn, listening out for the creaking branches, the tapping rain and my mama's easy breathing. She'd say:

Close your eyes, little lamb. Only the owls are awake at this time.

I'm sorry for dredging up old memories again. I was telling you about the bed, the sheets, the frayed fabric. If you want to plump a pillow well you have to give it a good smack. You have to smack the cushions too, and the curtains, and the rugs. Smack your palms together after carrying the heavy shopping bags. Give the watermelons and melons a quick smack to make sure you're choosing the sweetest ones. Smack your chest in church. Smack your cheeks when unreality strikes. A good beating is the only way to get the dust out and some air between the feathers. And I puffed those pillows every morning. They were full of air, those pillows where the señor and señora laid their heads at night.

At three days old, the baby finally cried. The señora was feeding her in bed with the window wide open. I know because I was sweeping the hallway and the fluff and dust kept flying about, caught in the draught. She called me from her bedroom and, in a whisper, asked me to take her a cup of camomile tea.

I was walking into her room with the tray when the girl suddenly started choking. She made a hollow, breathy sound and then, suddenly, nothing. The silence was terrifying. The girl couldn't breathe. The air simply wasn't getting through and her face was growing redder and redder. The señora shook her and thumped her on the back, but it was no use.

Cristóbal! she screamed.

It was a desperate cry. The señor was busy in his study. He'd asked not to be disturbed. He was working on a difficult case. He had to decide whether or not there was any point in treating this patient, whether to try to save her, a young woman, he'd said, shutting himself away with his papers. Luckily he heard the señora's scream.

He ran into the room, grabbed the girl, turned her upside down and violently shook her. A white trickle of vomit fell onto the rug. The girl began to cry, mouth open, face red, her arms stiff at her sides. How she cried. The señor passed her back to the señora.

Change position, he said. And then:

I'm going to the clinic, it's impossible to work here.

The señora tried to calm her daughter down, to soothe her, but it was no use. Each time she put her to the breast the girl would crane her head the other way and wail, beside herself. I was still there, you understand. Still holding the tray with the chamomile tea, silent and unmoving, I looked on as that baby screamed at the slightest contact with her mother's body. And at that point the señora looked at me, I remember it perfectly well. She looked at me, then at the stain on the floor, then back at me. She didn't say a single word. She didn't have to. I placed the tray on her night-stand and came back with a cloth.

All of this is important. Don't think I'm trying to buy time. Making the bed, airing the rooms, scrubbing the vomit out of the rug. I've told you before: you have to skirt around the edge before getting to the heart of the story. And do you know what's at the core of a story like this? Socks black with dirt, shirts with blood stains on them, an unhappy little girl, a woman keeping up appearances and a man keeping count: of every minute, every peso, every conquest. A man who wakes up before sunrise to squeeze in a jog, who brushes his teeth while sorting his things, who checks his diary while jogging, who reads the paper while eating. The type of person who lives his life according to a plan and knows exactly how every hour, every minute will be filled. Because the hours and minutes are part of that plan.

Nothing in the señor's life had ever thrown him off course. Not even his mother's death, years ago, though the sadness of it had apparently etched a few wrinkles at the corners of his eyes. Not even the arguments he had with his wife, although they did put him off his food. Not even that obstinate daughter of his, who refused to eat. His plan was ticking along nicely: study medicine, get married, buy a house, find it wanting. Sell the house, buy a bigger one, run into problems with the boss. Become the boss, produce a daughter, save lives, lose others. Then, having reached the top, slip up and say too much. I'll tell you all about this too, don't worry. I know you're on the edge of your seats. One morning the señor said too much and reality reared its head and snatched his plan clean away.

A few months after the birth, the señora announced she'd be returning to work. She told me she was going out, for a couple of hours, give or take. She needed to buy some new suits and a travel case for a trip to the south. She worked in the timber industry, did you know that? Paper, pine, paper, more pine. She had files and files of papers all related to pine: planed pine, the sale of sawdust, cut timber, the buying of land. The disadvantage of having a literate maid. She reads documents that don't concern her, written secrets: how much they earn, how much they spend, how much they'll inherit. But I've lost my thread again. I was telling you that the señora went off shopping and I, ever obedient, stayed at home alone.

What am I saying, 'alone'. I mean I stayed at home with the girl. I don't know when I first considered being with her as *not* being alone. I suppose that's an important moment, but it passed me by.

The señora was out for too long and the girl started to cry. By then she was six months old and she had an insatiable appetite. Later on, meals became a full-blown battle: it would take hours just to make her eat a couple of peas, accept two grains of rice. That day I tried feeding her sugar water, but it didn't work. She threw the bottle on the floor and her crying escalated to screaming. There was no formula in the house, the señora was still breastfeeding, so I decided to mash up a banana, cross my fingers and hope for the best. The girl devoured it and soon after fell asleep.

On her return, the señora noticed the dirty plate on the kitchen worktop and gave me a suspicious look. She very rarely looked at me, you know. I could be in the kitchen, her bedroom, or raking in the back garden. I could be anywhere in the house but she never looked at me. That day, though, she did. She wasn't happy that the maid had given the girl her first taste of fruit, so she fixed me with a glare, her face red with rage. I told you before that she was quick to turn red: red because I cut the girl's fringe, red because I sent her to her bedroom, red because the girl only ate if the maid did the airplane. She gave me a talking-to and I took it in silence. What was I supposed to say? She'd been out for nearly three hours, the girl had been screaming her head off and now she was sound asleep in her cot.

The señora immediately regretted her outburst. It doesn't pay to reproach the home help. A woman with access to the food, to the family secrets. She realised her error and tried to make amends.

Estelita, she said. Come and see what I bought.

The dress came in a box tied with a blue satin ribbon.

I bought it on sale, she said.

That's what I work for, she said.

That's what Señora Mara López worked for.

She stood in front of me and held the dress up against her body. The black, shiny fabric rested against her still-flabby stomach.

What do you think? she asked.

The dress was short and close-fitting. In it, her varicose veins would show, the waistband of her knickers digging into her hips would show.

It's nice, I said.

She smiled and asked me to go and hang it up.

The señora stayed downstairs, making herself a cup of tea, and I went off to her bedroom. I opened the wardrobe, took the dress out of its box and, without thinking, held it up against my apron. Some sequins I hadn't noticed before flashed in the mirror. But it wasn't enough for me. Before I knew what I had done, I'd taken off my uniform and put on the dress.

The fabric was silky, sheer, a sparkling black that glinted here and there. It was so soft that at any moment it seemed it might disappear, and I with it. Placing my hand on my waist I stared at my reflection. I looked common, dressed up like that. Common in that little black dress and my shabby plimsolls. It felt like the fabric was on fire and searing my skin.

I didn't hear the señora coming up the hall. I didn't hear her enter the room either. I only realised she was standing in the doorway when at last she spoke up.

Estela, she said.

At that point in time she was calling me Estelita. Bring me a fan, Estelita. My slippers, Estelita. A decaf coffee, no sugar, Estelita. Now, it was Estela.

I didn't know what to say. How was I supposed to reply? García? No, I didn't say anything. I waited for her to turn around, to stop looking at me, but I quickly realised that the señora had no intention of going anywhere. I would have to undress in front of her, like all those times she'd undressed in front of me, as if her maid couldn't see her rashy armpits, the ingrown hairs on her inner thighs, her post-partum belly.

Taking the dress by the hem I pulled it over my head then stood there in my knickers and bra, staring directly into her brown eyes. Plain, expressionless eyes. Then, as I stared at her, a thought came into my head. Write this down on your notepads, you'll like this. It came to me in a flash, an explosion of sound, an idea so deafening that I'm almost telling you just to be rid of it.

I wanted to see her dead.

That's right. I told you I wouldn't lie to you. That was what I wanted in that moment, and yet I didn't say a word. I didn't *do* anything, either, don't worry. The señora is alive and well. Bending down, I picked up my uniform and put it on as quickly as I could. Then I carefully smoothed out her dress and made some room for it in her wardrobe. And as I scrabbled around in her skirts looking for a damn hanger, the señora stopped me and said:

You'd better wash it first, Estela.

The girl, like all newborns, grew with dizzying speed. The same speed with which we age. But we prefer to ignore that. From one day to the next she could hold her head up, her hands could hold her own toys and her gums revealed another tiny white tooth. And one day around then, just a regular day, she said her first word.

She was sitting in her highchair and I was leaning in close trying to get her to eat. In the background, very quietly, the news was showing a man who'd set fire to himself outside a bank. His body blazed on the screen, a red-hot coal on its knees. His house had been repossessed because of some unpaid medical bills. His wife had died of cancer. He'd been left homeless and widowed. Set fire to himself, the news-reader said. Self-immolated, dead. The girl was staring at the fire when the señora walked into the kitchen and turned off the television.

The nana shouldn't be filling your head with all that tragedy, she said, or something like that, I don't remember.

With the TV switched off the girl became restless and began struggling in her seat. She babbled something, raised her arms in the air, shouted, spat and then suddenly fell quiet. Her eyes scanned the room as if looking for something on the walls, something lost on the shelves, until finally, apparently having found it, she pointed at me with her tiny forefinger. I saw the determination in her eyes and her mouth open to pronounce two identical syllables.

Na-na, she said, confidently.

That's how the señora referred to me, I suppose that's obvious: it's time for your bath with the nana, go and eat lunch with the nana, the nana will warm up your bottle.

The señora heard her. I did too. And both of us wanted the girl to not say another word, to go back to watching the man being burned alive on the screen. I held a spoonful of baby food to her mouth, but the girl, riveted by the miracle that was pointing and speaking, shouted 'Na-na, Na-na' at full volume.

The señora stared at her and for a few seconds she didn't know what to do. Her face was fixed in a grimace. Eventually she snatched her handbag and took out her phone.

Cristóbal, that's what she said.

She was calling the señor. She spoke in that specific tone of voice she used when she was either lying or furious: fractionally higher than usual. I carried on, feeding the baby bigger and bigger spoonfuls to bury the words in her throat. But by now she was shouting 'Nana!' and on the verge of tears.

The señora's voice became louder and more high-pitched. I could tell she was agitated. She licked her lips and swallowed. At first she faltered, as if unable to find the words. Then she let it all spill out, telling her husband how little Julia had spoken for the first time, so precocious, so advanced for her age, and guess what her first word was, guess what she said, Cristóbal, go on, have a guess …

Her first word was 'Mama'.

That's what the señora said.

I think we'll continue in the morning. That's all for today.

It's hard to know which event took place in the first year, which in the second, which in the third. It's hard to tell before from after, one summer from the next. Her first word, her first solid food, her first tantrum. Having an order would help me organise the story better. Then I could go step by step, hour by hour, without jumping from one fact to another, from one idea to the next.

She sucked her thumb, the girl. She would suck it furiously while staring blankly into space. I sometimes wondered what must be going through that little head of hers. Maybe she was going back over the illustrations from her children's books, or maybe a child's thoughts are nothing more than shapes and colours. The señora hated her daughter sucking her thumb. The moment the girl started moving it towards her mouth she would slap her wrist.

No, she would say. And then:

You'll get buck teeth, Julita. And do you know what little girls with buck teeth look like? Ugly, that's what.

The girl, who had gaps between her milk teeth, would stare open-mouthed at her thumb, shiny with spit. And soon after, without her realising, it would be back in her mouth.

She was very pretty during that period. She was pretty later on, too, but had become too thin, pale, spiritless. As a baby, on the other hand, she was chubby and cheerful. She would crawl around the house and climb up my legs while I mopped the floor. Or she'd knock on the frosted glass to get me to go and look at a spider, a woodlouse, or a black cat perched on the dividing wall with the neighbours.

Initially she could only drag herself with her arms across the floor and the señora would tease her. The snake, she called her, and we'd both laugh. Pretty soon she learned to crawl, although that phase was short-lived. A few weeks at most, and then she was walking.

The señora was sitting in an armchair looking at her phone when the girl, who was playing with some puzzles on the floor, grabbed one of the armrests and pulled herself up to standing. It happened quickly. From sitting to standing and, out of nowhere, two quick steps. I saw it as I was taking some queso fresco on toast to the señora.

The girl's walking! I almost shouted.

The señora looked up. The girl was still on her feet, surprised at herself. She took one more short step before falling to the floor, where she stayed. She started to laugh: sweet, gentle chuckles. She looked at me with that easy, infectious laugh of hers, that laugh which no longer exists. The señora picked her up, hugged her and twirled her around like a spinning top. One turn, another turn, to the sound of their laughter. I watched them from a few metres away. The daughter, her mother, that dance, happy and complete.

With her first steps came her first check-up. The señor put his daughter in her highchair, took off her socks and examined her feet. Her ten toes, then the soles, backs and arches. Two perfect little girl's feet, I thought while I cooked. The señor didn't agree.

She has your feet, he told the señora, who was putting the shopping away in the larder.

Flat, collapsed arches, she'll need insoles.

Next it was her eyes. He thought it important to take the girl to the ophthalmologist as soon as possible. He said infant myopia was out of control. He used those words, out of control, while I mushed her food. It was her favourite: chicken, potatoes, pumpkin.

He continued his examination. He held her arms and lifted them up. Next he gave her thighs a squeeze. At that point he turned around and asked me how much food I fed her.

A serving like this, I said, showing him the bowl with little pictures on it.

And for dessert?

Fruit.

How much?

I didn't answer. The señora was also there. They were both looking at the maid, appraising her replies.

She's getting fat, the señor said. And then:

You must keep a check on her diet, Estela. Childhood obesity is out of control.

That, too, was out of control. Obesity. Myopia. The girl looked at him and started to cry. A piercing, irritating cry. The señor picked her up and tried to soothe her. Howls. Screams. The señora took her from him. Kicks, punches. Out of control, I thought, but I didn't say a word.

The señora, though, did speak:

You take her, Estela.

I took the girl out into the back garden. It was spring, I remember it well, but unseasonably warm. The girl was still kicking and screeching in my ear as I tried to think of a children's song. It was no good, I couldn't hear my thoughts over her screams. I walked in circuits around the pool with her in my arms. I had the idea to distract her with the trees.

This is a fig tree, I said. When you're big you're going to climb it.

This is a magnolia, I went on.

A plum.

A camellia.

My mama taught me the names of the trees, if you're wondering how I know them. I learned them all on a single winter's morning. There'd been a storm, a tree had fallen into the road and the bus that was taking me home couldn't go any further.

Everyone off here, the driver said, and he left us there, stranded.

I must have been eight or nine, no older than that, and I was forced to cross open countryside, in the rain, without an umbrella. My shoes sank into the mud, the wind whistled in my ears, the branches of the trees above me were bowing right down to the ground. In my memory I walked for hours, but I don't actually know how long it was. I arrived home hungry and soaked to the bone. My mama told me to take my clothes off, then she wrapped me in a woollen poncho. Drying my hair with a towel she asked me just one question.

What kind of tree was it, Lita?

I shrugged. To me it was just a tree, a great big trunk lying slap in the middle of the road, a tree with branches and leaves, like all the other trees. My mama insisted.

What did the trunk look like? What colour was it? How thick was it, Lita?

The next day she woke me up at the crack of dawn and took me out for a walk. She showed me the maple, the raulí, the cypress, the pehuén, the arrayán, the ulmo. She touched each trunk with her palm, as if baptising the tree. I had to repeat the names and touch each trunk too. Then she showed me how to tell a maqui from a voqui, a myrtle, a raspberry. Once she'd finished, she locked eyes with me.

Names are important, she said. Your friends have names, don't they, Lita? You don't call them 'girl' and 'boy', do you? Would you call a cow 'animal'?

By the time I'd finished showing the girl all the trees in the garden, she had calmed down. She touched their leaves gently. She looked carefully at the twigs, the crowns and the foliage, dusty from the lack of rain. I took her back into the kitchen to give her lunch and the señor and señora were no longer there. I put her in her highchair, looked at her feet and kissed them both.

Podgy paws, I said.

She laughed, happy again. I served her a big bowl of food, which she devoured. I heard the bathroom door close. Then the front door. Once I was sure they weren't coming back, I opened the fridge, took out the blackberry jam, placed it on her highchair table, took her hand and slathered her thumb in the jam. The girl looked at her sticky black finger and understood. Smiling, she raised it to her lips. She sucked her thumb all day long.

I know what you must be thinking: how ungrateful. I had food, work, a roof over my head and clothes on my back. I had a monthly income. Something like a home. And they treated me well, I can't lie. Not a raised voice in seven years.

It's true they argued sometimes. Quarrels about nursery, potential schools and if it was a good idea for their daughter to play with the Gómez girl, filthy, snotty little thing that she was. Other times they argued about money. Money spent on expensive shirts, designer suits and Italian shoes, when the plan was to save for a second home in a beach town with a sea view. They never shouted though. Not ever. The odd slammed door and objection muttered under their breath, which only I heard.

After their fights the señora liked to tidy up. She'd organise her papers, her files, fold the already-folded bed linen, take her blouses from her wardrobe and arrange them by colour. When something displeased her, whatever it might be, her face would turn red.

Don't touch my papers, Estela.

Did you take the blue file?

I'm going to show you how to fold underwear: one side, then the other, then the bottom, like that.

Did you dust the skirting boards or do you want me to die from my allergies?

Once, she removed all her shoes from the wardrobe, dozens of pairs lined up on the terrace, and she polished them one by one. They looked like new.

Now that's how you shine a shoe, she said afterwards, her hands black with polish.

When the girl was precisely two years old her parents thought it time to start socializing her. That was the word the señor used as they finished eating dessert in the dining room. I overheard the conversation while I dried the dishes, the deep bowls for the soup, and the shallow ones for the main course.

The señora said:

Isn't she a little young?

And the señor:

What do you want? For her to spend all day with Estela?

The señor said that these were decisive years. Children who didn't go to nursery fell behind at school.

She's exactly the right age, he said. We have to think about her future.

The señora nodded, or I think she did.

A few days later they explained to their daughter that she was going to start nursery. The girl was toddling from here to there, the señor and señora trying to block her path.

You'll be a good girl, the señor said. You'll be the smartest little girl there.

They showed her the sky-blue checked pinafore she'd have to wear. Different from mine, don't worry. Hers had real buttons all the way down the front and a lace trim to adorn the neck of their pretty girl. I embroidered her name onto the front pocket myself: J-U-L-I-A. She would attend from 8 a.m. to noon, Monday through Friday, starting the following month. The girl looked at them for a moment, at her father, at her mother, then raised one hand to her mouth. I thought she was going to start sucking her thumb, but that isn't what happened. Instead, she turned her thumb around, examined the nail and carefully chewed off the edge. The señora gave her a slap on the wrist.

Absolutely not, I draw the line.

The señor let it pass. He would later come to worry about that compulsion of hers, the anxiousness with which she put her fingers in her mouth. They couldn't control it. The bitten-down nails, the bleeding cuticles, her rigour and meticulousness as she moved from one finger to the next, from one hand to the next.

That night, as on so many other nights, I couldn't sleep. I kept thinking about the girl, about her nails, about the sudden grownupness of that gesture, about her chubby, idle hands, always ready to pop those nails into her mouth, for them to be destroyed by her teeth. I never bit my nails. My mama didn't either. I suppose for that you'd need to have your hands free.

I know what you'll say:

The events were brought about by a lack of sleep.

You'll write:

Insomnia caused confusion, hallucinations, brief outbursts of hatred.

You'll conclude:

She stopped being able to distinguish night from day, an order from a favour, reality from fantasy.

But make no mistake about it: I've never had any fantasies. There's reality and there's unreality, just like there's the dead and the living, what's relevant and what isn't, but I'll come to that later.

That night I was gasping with thirst; a thirst similar to the kind I feel now. As if the drought were inside of me, on the inside of my throat. I opened my eyes, turned and checked the time on my phone: 1:22 a.m. That meant it was 2:22 a.m. in the morning. I didn't want to put my clock on summer time. Only winter tells the truth, that's what my mama used to say as the rain pelted down on the other side of the window.

I sat up in bed and stretched out my hand to the nightstand. I put a glass of water there every night and would drink it sip by sip, hour after hour, until the glass was empty, and dawn finally broke. This time though, my hand only met with the table. This lapse terrified me. My hand expected the glass and the glass wasn't there. Then it occurred to me that perhaps I wasn't there either; that if a hand reached out to try to touch me it would find an empty space on the bed.

The contact of my feet against the floor tiles returned me to my own body, but I still couldn't shake the feeling of unease. I felt a searing thirst in my throat. Everyone in the house would be asleep, so I went barefoot and in my nightshirt to get a glass of water from the kitchen. I slid open the door and headed towards the larder. The kitchen was also in the dark but I noticed the dining-room light was on, and the door left ajar. I wondered if I myself had forgotten to close it.

I don't know how I didn't hear them. I suppose because I wasn't expecting to hear anything or see anyone. I pushed open the door and that's when I saw the señora. She was sitting stark naked, facing away from me, on the dining-room table with her legs wide open, lit by the yellow glow of the standing lamp. I could hear her laboured breathing, like that of a wounded animal, and I noticed her back was slightly arched. A back covered in moles, a tad flabby at the waist, with a red mark from where her tight bra had dug in during the day. Standing in front of her, with his eyes closed, was the señor. He had his trousers and pants down at his ankles but his pristine shirt was still buttoned up to the collar; the shirt I had ironed for him first thing that morning.

I stood absolutely still, unsure what to do. If I didn't move, if I didn't breathe, perhaps they wouldn't see me. What doesn't move blends in, my mama used to say, looking at the brown-spotted owl camouflaging itself against the cinnamon tree. And so, although still thirsty, I didn't move. My eyes were glued to that man: his taut, flushed skin, his parted lips, his furrowed brow and eyelids squeezed together so tightly it looked like his eyes had sunk into his face. He was humping his wife with a certain tedium, in and out, in and out as his expression grew increasingly twisted. The señora didn't see me at any point; her eyes were looking at the opposite wall. But the señor's eyes, that man's eyes, suddenly opened. He spotted me, I'm sure he did, but that didn't stop him. He stayed where he was, in his dining room, fucking his wife.

I know you won't transcribe that word, that you'll play the prudes, but it's the best word to describe what was happening before my eyes: the husband fucking his wife, part-absent, part-furious, back and forth with increasing exasperation. And she sat there on the table like a statue, legs splayed, neck tensed, her back about to snap in two.

I took a step back, dazed, not entirely sure whether I was even awake or could make it to the back room or that I wouldn't die of thirst right there, just a few paces from the kitchen and the tap with its drip, drip, drip, like a taunt. And as I retreated, the floor creaked and he stopped and saw me. This time I didn't doubt it. First my face, but then his eyes moved down to my feet. And with his gaze fixed on his housemaid's feet, on the ten toes that were now forming a damp imprint on the floor, he began to move desperately, moaning and groaning even more loudly.

I turned around without a glass, without any water to quench my thirst, without any sense of whether upon re-entering the back room I would find the other woman on the bed, the one who in the morning would rub furniture polish into that table, the scorching iron over that shirt, mole removal creams into her employer's back. I slid open the door, closed it again and saw that it was still dark in there, as dark as before. I quickly got under the sheets and tried to sleep. For once, to sleep until the next day, the next year, the next life.

Over on the other side of the door, the moans were getting louder, his deeper and longer, hers higher-pitched and breathier. A warm feeling rushed through me; a sudden, revulsive heat that crept up my legs from my feet. The same feet on which he'd locked his wild eyes. The bare feet of his housemaid where they made contact with the floor. The heat climbed up the bridges of my feet, spread along my calves, expanded across my now soft, warm thighs. I opened my legs. The heat was still there. Outside, moaning. Inside, silence. I turned onto my front, my face pressed against the pillow and that thirst like a deep crack running from my throat to my belly. I put my fingers in my mouth until they were warm and wet. And there, with my eyes closed, with that interminable thirst, the darkness and urgency deep inside of me, I touched myself, harder, faster.

I didn't see the señora the next morning. She left for work without saying goodbye and called me at around three.

Estela, make a note of this, she said.

Educated, hard-working, a discreet maid.

I was to defrost the chicken breasts and stuff them with spinach and toasted almonds. I should also make roast potatoes and prepare a round of dry pisco sours.

Nothing like a homemade pisco sour, she said, as if she were talking to someone else.

The señora wanted to know if I knew the measures. I told her I did, but she repeated them to me anyway. Three times she warned me not to overdo it on the sugar.

Nothing worse than a sweet pisco sour, she said.

After that she asked me if I could go to the supermarket.

Estelita, she said, can you get angostura bitters, lemons and organic eggs?

She asked me as if it were in my power to say no. To say: Señora, do you know what? I won't be going, I don't feel like it, I didn't sleep last night after seeing you and your husband fucking in the dining room.

I felt something hard on my neck, like a stone, right there, on the softest part of my body. And I saw her again on the table, her back to me, naked, legs wide open, but instead of her feet, my own.

That morning I had swept the floor and polished the furniture. I'd changed the sheets and towels and washed down the pavement in front of the house. And in a few hours guests would be arriving for dinner. I would have liked a bit more warning, that's all. I'd have left the polishing for later, preserved my energy. But what did my energy matter to her? Buttoned lips, dependable, I left for the supermarket.

Outside, the heat flooded my whole body. A dry, harsh heat, from which there was no escape. I longed for the cold of the south, for the sound of the rain on the roof, but my daydreaming was interrupted by the guy who manned the petrol pump. On seeing me he raised his eyebrows, waved and smiled, showing his small, square teeth. The smile of a good man, my mama would say. The dog at his side also looked at me. With her dull coat and gluey eyes, she looked like any other stray.

Hey, the man said, as if he already knew me.

Lost in my thoughts of the past, I didn't know how to respond, and I made a clumsy gesture like a curtsey. I felt my face blush and my mouth was as dry as it is now. He seemed to realise and his smile grew even wider.

Do you collect them? he asked.

He'd been spying on me and now he wanted to know what I'd been looking for on the ground. Why I kept bending down and putting handfuls of stones in my pocket.

Something like that, I replied, and I carried on past him.

I was several metres away when I heard his voice again.

See you around, he said, and I kept walking, faster now.

I'd forgotten about our encounter by the time I got back to the house. I could only think about the weight of the stones in my apron pocket. Oval, perfect stones, neither too big nor too small. Like the ones my mama used to collect on the beach and then throw to the bottom of the sea. She took care selecting them, taking some, leaving others. She liked skimming the flat ones, making them bounce off towards the horizon. The bigger ones she would keep and take home. White, grey, black, striped. They must still be there, on the window ledge, as if gazing out to sea. The stones in my uniform, on the other hand, were bumping against one another, clack, clack, clack, at the bottom of my pocket. I left them there and got to work preparing dinner, using the tip of the knife to score a line along the chicken breasts, then using my fingers to tear the cartilage from the flesh. In the middle of each one, I carefully pressed the spinach and toasted almond stuffing I'd prepared before going out.

Hello?

What's the matter?

I thought I heard a noise over there. Was that a yawn? I'm like a recipe book, am I? Well, good, because that was my life: chicken, cartilage, checking the potatoes weren't sticking to the baking dish, checking the madness wasn't sticking to the inside of my skull, checking my eyes weren't popping out of their sockets. I washed the potatoes and, without removing their skin, cut them into very fine slices. Next I distributed them evenly across the ceramic baking dish, splashed them with olive oil, and added some rosemary and salt. At exactly 7:40 in the evening I would put the chicken in the oven. At eight I would add the potatoes. And it would all be ready at eight thirty. If the guests arrived on time, they could be sitting at their places eating by eight forty-five, dessert at nine thirty, the digestif at ten, the dishes washed by ten thirty, the kitchen swept and mopped and I'd be in bed by close to eleven.

The bell rang on cue. The señora wanted to know if the pisco sours were ready. She'd asked me to make them at the very last minute.

They won't be frothy otherwise, she said.

Not too sweet, she repeated, twice, three times.

I took down the blender from the shelf and into it I put the measures of pisco, lemon, sugar, ice and egg whites. Obedient, servile, a maid with a fine touch. On the other side I heard the hellos and the usual questions: the girl's age, school, the weather, work. With every answer I took another stone from my pocket. They made a heavy plop as they hit the liquid, then sank to the bottom of the blender, among hundreds of tiny bubbles. They looked very pretty down there. Like stones in a yellow sea. I could have stared at them for a long time if I hadn't been in a hurry. Always such a hurry. I put the lid on, placed my hand on it, turned the dial to full power and, without a second thought, pressed the button.

On the other side of the door a tense silence fell, soon replaced by the girl's screaming. The noise had been loud, like an explosion, and had woken her up. I heard the señor go to her room to settle her. The señora said:

I won't be a minute; I'll just go and see what happened.

A wash of yellow liquid was dripping from the edge of the kitchen worktop. My uniform was completely soaked in alcohol. On the floor, at my feet, among the broken glass and the ice, the stones were still intact, just as perfect as before. I picked them up, dried them with a cloth, and put them back in my pocket.

The señora entered the kitchen.

What happened? she asked.

She saw the broken glass on the floor, the pisco sour spilled everywhere, the irretrievable aperitif. Clumsy, careless, a butterfingered maid. She couldn't see the stones, or that's what I thought.

She settled down then and told me not to worry, it was an old blender, about time they replaced it.

Are you okay, Estela?

I nodded in silence, with that weight in my pockets. The señora went over to the fridge and took out a bottle of champagne, but then stopped in her tracks. From behind I watched her shoulders stiffen and I could almost see the redness of her face travelling around to the back of her neck. She bent her head down to the floor. There, at her feet, was a shiny wet stone. She saw it and understood, of course she understood. Bending down slowly, she picked it up from the floor. When she turned around I could finally see her flushed skin and the involuntary twitch in her left eyelid. She placed the stone on the kitchen worktop and stared directly at me. I wish I could describe her expression for you, but I wouldn't know how. Think of a word to describe a mixture of surprise and contempt.

The silence lasted for a few seconds, not too long. Outside, her guests were waiting for her, a couple of senior players from the company. She needed to calm down, go back out there, keep her composure. In her high-pitched voice, through gritted teeth, the señora spoke up.

I'll dock the blender from your pay, she said.

Immediately afterwards she straightened up, patted down her skirt and returned to her guests, crying:

Cheers, everybody. Cheers.

By now you're probably wondering why I stayed. It's a good question, one of those important questions. Do you feel sad? Are you happy? You know the sort of thing. My answer is the following: Why do you stay in your jobs? In your poky offices, in the factories, in the shops on the other side of this wall?

I never stopped believing I would leave that house, but routine is treacherous; the repetition of the same rituals – open your eyes, close them, chew, swallow, brush your hair, brush your teeth – each one an attempt to gain mastery over time. A month, a week, the length and breadth of a life.

The señora deducted the cost of the blender from my pay, then got over the *impasse*. That's what she said, 'Estela, I'm over that *impasse*.' And for my part, at some point between cooking dinner and putting her daughter to bed, I made my decision. A month. In a month's time I would go back to the land to hear rain crashing against the corrugated zinc roof. Rather there than here, rather in company than alone, rather the cold than the heat, rather rain than drought. I hadn't saved up enough to do the extensions on my mama's house, to build a new bedroom or a new bathroom for me, but what did it matter? I'd get a job at the bakery or picking seaweed for the Japanese. Or even, if need be, on the salmon farms. Then my mama would say: Nuh uh, Lita, no way, anything but that. Those people pay late, badly or never. They feed those poor critters poison and then they wonder why, after working there, the workers get sick and drop down dead.

I thought about it for several days. I had to get out of there, by whatever means necessary.

I think the decision alone did it. It was enough for me to have made up my mind for reality to strike back. My phone rang.

Hello? That's what I said.

And at the other end of the line:

Estela.

It was my cousin Sonia. She told me my mama had had a fall. She'd been up the apple tree and the branch had snapped, along with the bone connecting my mama's hip to her knee. Money, Sonia kept repeating. She needed money to take her from the sticks to the clinic, from the clinic to the hospital, from the hospital to the pharmacy. Money so she could take time off to look after my mama.

I was alone in the kitchen. The señor had taken the girl out for a walk. The señora was at the gym. It wasn't long until Christmas, when I'd have a holiday. Two weeks off. I was going to travel south. Even if it was raining there. Even if it was cold. Even if there wasn't enough money to buy food. Even if the rain came dripping through the roof onto the floor. Even if the wood was rotting. I could almost smell the salty trace of the sea breeze. Almost see the feverish yellow of the gorse along the road. That was the moment, I suppose. The moment I should have left, telling Sonia:

I'm coming home, I'll be there tomorrow.

And the señora:

I quit.

But instead I looked up and cast my eyes around the room, at the walls, at the fruit bowl overflowing with figs, at the steam calmly rising out of the tea pot, at the mug ready to receive the freshly boiled water. And I could picture my mama. My mama filling a mug with boiling water and putting her index finger and thumb into it to pull out the tea bag as quickly as possible in order to reuse it for the next cup of tea. And I would watch her, not understanding how she didn't burn herself. Her fingers touching the water, red but numb. As the years went by, I came to understand. Now I, too, can sink my fingers into just-boiled water.

I began to transfer her money on the thirtieth of every month. Almost all of my salary directly into my cousin Sonia's account. And my mama slowly started walking again, albeit with a limp. And the señora returned to her job and I remained there, trapped in mine. And the Christmases and New Years went by and the girl grew in years. And I, meanwhile, I guess I just got used to it.

Actually, maybe that's not the right word for it. Cross that out, please. What happened to me was something else: the thing about the fingers in the boiling water ... that's it, that's it, that's it.

Sometimes I'd lie there in the middle of the night wondering which memories she'd hold on to. The girl I mean, who else? The dead girl who's got us all caught up in this mess. I know it doesn't matter anymore, but sometimes, after I'd bathed her, dried her hair and got her into her pyjamas, after I'd tidied up her toys and kissed her goodnight, I would ask myself whether she'd remember me when I was no longer there.

I can recall, very clearly, the first time I travelled from Chiloé to Santiago. I remember thinking that the air smelled of dust, that it was incredibly hot and that the city only had two colours: yellow and brown. Yellow trees, brown hills; yellow buildings, brown squares. Back in those days I would amuse myself playing little games like that one: naming the main colours, repeating words, counting the animals I spotted in the wild. I also remember, from that trip, going up a steep hillside, also yellow and brown, on a cable car. I was so gripped by vertigo you would have thought I was all on my own up there. The cabin lurched back and forth and my heart was in my mouth. My mama was next to me, holding my hand, but my fear somehow erased her. In my memory I'm alone, suspended under a brown sky and over a yellow city, where I was about to die.

The girl would probably remember eating chicken and mashed potato for supper, being warm and clean and wearing her hair in a French plait. Clearest of all she'd remember how that plait pinched the skin at the back of her neck, and the hands that would separate her hair into three sections before weaving them together, one after the other. Maybe, who knows, she would even remember my hands, just like I remember my mama's sturdy hands. My mama standing paralysed on a dirt road having spotted a pack of wild dogs approaching. My mama crouching down on that track, where we were alone, holding out her hand to each of those creature's muzzles in turn. Her palm facing down and slack before those razor-sharp fangs. The quick sniff, the moment of doubt, the friendly lick. She taught me that trick, my mama. Hold out a gentle hand to demonstrate submissiveness.

No, of course the girl wouldn't remember me. But maybe, had she lived, she'd have remembered my hands.

I slept with her, with my mama, until I was seven. It's a strange coincidence, because it's like my childhood memories all mounted up until my seventh birthday and then, poof, disappeared. My mama was a day maid in a big villa in Ancud. She'd leave our home at dawn and return at ten at night, bleary-eyed, panting at the door. Really it was more like grunting. And grunting away she would take off her raincoat, sweatshirt and mud-splattered trousers. I would pretend to be asleep and spy on her, paying particular attention to her navel. I was fascinated by that button hidden in the folds of her skin. Having undressed down to her knickers and bra, she would take a piece of cotton wool dipped in lavender water. And so began her ritual. She would wipe that cotton wool across her forehead, her cheeks, down her neck, arms and over the palms of her hands, and then take another one and run it over her armpits, the backs of her knees and between her thighs and toes. It took a long time to apply those cotton wool balls to every last bit of her skin. And I would watch her from the bed and wonder what the surface area of her body might be; if perhaps my mama was rubbing those cotton wool balls over a space as big as the room. As wide as the land. As long as the map of the country that hung from the blackboard at school.

By the time she'd finished, the waste basket would be full of filthy cotton wool. Then my mama would put on her white pyjamas and slide in between the sheets. I would lie in bed waiting for her, awake but with my eyes closed. I always wanted her to tell me something about her day but now I understand why she never said a word. What could she possibly tell me? Within seconds she'd be sound asleep: the whole of my mama resting, except for her hands. Her fingers would stay awake all night. They'd jerk, tremble and tap the mattress, as if they couldn't stop working, as if they no longer knew how to rest.

You're losing your patience … is that it? Have you got cramp in your fingers? Have your bums gone numb on your seats? Are you biting your cuticles over there anxiously awaiting cause of death? This is a long story, my friends, as you'll have worked out for yourselves. It predates me and you; it predates even my mama or yours. It's a story born of a centuries-old tiredness and questions that presume too much. Or have any of you ever been asked if you feel tenderly towards your superiors? If you love your boss, your supervisor, the staff manager? I cleaned their house, dusted their furniture, made sure there was a hot plate of food waiting for them in the evenings. Those things have nothing to do with love.

The beds were made each day. What am I saying, 'were made'? I made the beds each day, although 'made' isn't the right word either. Make the fire, make up the spare room … as if I were the one inventing them.

Mondays were reserved for deep cleaning and the routine went like this: open the living-room doors leading out into the garden and start with the ceiling lamps. Rock them gently with the feather duster and watch the spray of golden particles rain down. It's important to work from the top of the room downwards and let all the dust fall to the ground. Then shake out the cushions, scrub the side tables, wipe the dust off the leaves of the rubber plant. After that, only at the end: sweep, mop, wax and polish. And a week later, begin all over again.

I'm telling you about my Mondays. Have I gone too far? I heard groaning over there. You want only the relevant action, do you? The stuff that drives the story onwards? Well I'm not here to entertain you. I'm not trying to be smart. The beginning is Monday, the glass coffee table: lifting up the ashtray, the porcelain urn, the art book and vase. Polishing each object in turn and placing them, for the time being, on the sofa. At that point the only thing on the table's translucent surface is the secret message left by those objects: two medium-sized spheres, one small square, one large rectangle. The dust murmured that message every seven days. And under the rugs and behind the paintings, the same enigma, left there for me to decipher.

But I've gone way off course again, like when insects fly too low and end up splattered on a windscreen. I thought I heard you on the other side of the glass. I'm talking to you, you over there taking notes, you who'll eventually pass judgement on me. My voice bothers you, doesn't it? Let's talk about that, about my voice. You were expecting something else, isn't that right? A meeker, more grateful sort of voice. Are you writing all these words down? Are you recording my digressions? What's wrong now? The maid can't use the word 'digressions', either? Could you show me the list of your words and mine?

I had a little game whenever I went out to do the shopping in which I had to name all the different kinds of mouths on the passers-by: cheerful, angry, distraught, neutral. Edges turned up, edges turned down. Mouths are always hiding something, even if most people don't pay much attention to them. Words leave their mark, sketch deep lines that can't be erased. Look at your own mouths if you don't believe me. At the marks left by judgemental words, by the cruel and unnecessary things you've said. And now look at my mouth with its thin, pink, perfectly smooth lips. The mouth of someone who has barely spoken a word … until now, of course.

But going back to my voice, the home help should speak other sorts of words, shouldn't she? In a harried, clumsy voice littered with dropped aitches and wide-open vowels. A voice that's different to all the others, to mark her out. To identify her even when she's not in uniform.

One day the girl said 'they was'. It wasn't even that long ago. Do you know this story? Since we're on the subject of words, I may as well tell you.

They was staying over, she said at dinner.

The señor almost had a heart attack.

It's 'they were', not 'they was'. Where did you pick that up?

The señor thought the girl had heard that phrase from me. That the maid spoke to his daughter in an unacceptable slang, in her dialect burdened with errors. All because once, just once, I made what he called 'a slip'.

I was giving the girl her bath. She never liked being washed. It was a real battle just to get her out of her clothes and into the tub. On that occasion, though, I managed it without too much trouble. Lifting her up, I let her feet lightly graze the water, and then sat her down. Three or four years old she must have been. The water reached her belly button.

Lie back, I told her. Let's get your hair wet.

She didn't move.

Lean your head back, niña, we need to have a wash if you're going to go to nursery.

Her body remained stiff, motionless. I realised she wasn't going to move. I tried leaning her forward and forcing her, but not even that worked. So I turned on the cold tap all the way, took the shower head and pointed it right in her face. She was shocked and closed her eyes and spluttered, but she didn't cry. This story really shouldn't horrify you. We all lose our cool sometimes. The girl remained still, completely drenched, holding me dangerously close to the limit of my patience as I lathered her hair and watched the suds run down her face. It must have stung her eyes. She must have choked and swallowed shampoo, but still she didn't move.

Just lift up your little arm, I said.

And again, nothing.

Lift up your arm, I repeated.

She didn't move a muscle.

I grabbed her hard by the wrist and yanked her arm up over her head.

I must have said: We'd better clean those dirty armpits, or, Your armpits are filthy, or, Let's see those stinky armpits. I don't know what I said. I only know that the señor overheard me and from the doorway said:

We don't say 'armpit', Estela. We say 'underarm'. Watch those slips.

So when the girl, years later at the dinner table, said the words 'they was' in front of her mother and father, the señor immediately called me into the dining room.

Estela, he said.

And then:

They *were*. The correct phrase is 'they were'.

All of this is important: whether the corners of a mouth turn up or down, sad mouths or smug mouths, the letters that form a word. The word 'rage', for example, has just four. Four little letters. And yet, my chest was burning.

Did you make a note of my age in your records? Estela García, forty years old, domestic worker. I'm sure you must have written down that description and then, behind my back, commented on this haggard face. The face of a sixty-year-old woman, of a one-hundred-and-twenty-million-year-old woman. The skin on my neck sagging, the first grey hairs showing at my temples, wrinkles here and there, eyes puffy with tiredness. But faces never tell the truth; don't be fooled. Faces pretend, lie, fake, cover up. And so the lines on a face are the lines of the most frequent lies, the courteous smiles and the countless sleepless nights.

The señora always spent a long time doing herself up in the mirror. She used creams, foundation, then more creams and powders that made her look pale, like a porcelain doll. The girl would sometimes watch her from the foot of the bed and copy her movements: eyebrows arched, lips puckered, eyelids half closed. As if she were trying out, one by one, the many faces she would put on in the future.

Once, she asked her mother why she didn't lend me some makeup.

To make her look white, she said.

Clean.

Meanwhile I got on with plumping the pillows or putting the folded pyjamas under the pillows or dusting the nightstands.

Faces lie, do you see? Hands don't have that option. The señora's smooth hands with their shiny painted nails and not a single callus, not one line despite her being several years older than me. The girl's restless hands, always finding their way to her mouth where her teeth would seek out any hard bits of skin and rip them till they bled. Take a look if you don't believe me. Compare your hands with mine. Look for burn marks on the backs of them, hardened grooves in the knuckles. Look at the texture of your palms.

One Sunday, not long after I'd arrived there, I decided to spend the whole day sleeping. I was tired, of course. And despondent. On the Saturday night I disabled my alarm and promised myself I would get some rest. I slept until my body couldn't sleep any longer, until it was all slept out. I opened my eyes at six in the morning. By seven I was up and dressed. By eight I was out of the house with nowhere to go. It's a funny thing, the body: a machine designed for routine.

More commonly, though, I chose not to go out on Sundays. I'd stay in the back room, sitting up in bed reading magazines, books, whatever I could find. Sometimes I'd call my mama. We'd talk for hours, and she'd tell me about her broken bone and how the rain made the pain worse and about the owl who'd been flying around the house ominously. I would just listen to her with my eyes closed, still and silent, and watch the images fly back and forth between her side of the world and mine.

She talked a lot about her childhood. It hadn't really occurred to me until now. I suppose there was little to say about either of our present circumstances, but in her childhood she used to eat ulpo made with toasted flour, milk and honey, stroke newborn calves and spot pudus in the wild. I don't know how much of it was true. My grandma had been widowed young and my mama was sent to work as a child. At fourteen she started working as a housemaid, and she never stopped. But in her memory she'd been happy: munching on the maqui berries that grew along the dirt road home, getting a shock in the evening when she looked in the mirror and saw her tongue stained black. We would both laugh at her stories, and it was real laughter. Something else real was how, as she spoke about the land, it would open out before me. I could almost hear the piglets squealing, the hens clucking, the cormorants flapping their wings, the horseflies bumping into the windows. And further away, in the distance, the dolphins jumping over the water's surface, the slow, steady sound of the waves. The same sound as the wind between the trees' framework. It felt like I could hear the clouds as they brushed past one another, smell the potatoes and tortillas on the coals of the open fire.

I don't know why once, years ago, back when I was a child, I'd interrupted one of her stories to ask about my father. A casual, unimportant question, as if I were asking how she'd slept or how her day had been. I don't think she'd seen it coming. For a long time she was silent, then she said:

Tell me, snotbag, have you ever wanted for anything?

I never asked her again.

On the island, as a child, I would spend my days alone. Actually, cross that out. I spent my days with the cows, the ducks, the dogs, the sheep. And of course that can't be called solitude. Somctimes I'd spend the afternoon reading. Old, weighty books that my mama would bring back from work when her employer was going to give them away. And then the neighbour had two kids my age. Jaime and his twin brother, who everyone also called Jaime. Stops us mixing them up, my mama would say, laughing her head off. Jaime and Jaime both worked on the ferry and had done since they were thirteen; day and night, night and day, back and forth between Pargua and Chacao. In the summer we would slash the tyres of the Santiago tourists' cars or throw duck eggs at their front windscreens. Other times the Jaimes would snap the necks of sparrows or even bite each other's necks playing vampires. From biting we soon moved on to kissing. I would kiss one Jaime, then the other, and then the Jaimes would kiss each other, like someone kissing a mirror. And meanwhile, we grew, just like the girl was growing. And my mama kept working in the big villa in Ancud, from dawn till dusk, she would say, even if the sun rose on her way there.

We left the house together, at six on the dot, she to go to work and I to school. Before going our separate ways, she would say: Have you got your hat, Lita? That was how she'd say goodbye as she went to get on the bus. Sometimes I'd be wearing my hat and even then she'd say: Don't forget your hat, trouble. The wind picks up in the afternoon, your ears will freeze. As far as my mama was concerned you caught all illnesses through your head, so I was to wear that wool hat and put up with the itchy rash it gave me. Sometimes, only sometimes, I would purposefully not wear it to get my mama to say: Where's your hat, chicken? I would run back to the house, put it on, and my mama would pat me on the head when I came back out. But if she ever forgot to ask, if she didn't turn to look at me before heading off to the bus stop, I would think, petrified: Today is a terrible day. I'm definitely going to die. And I would wait for the morning light to reveal the outlines of the mañío trees while I watched the lyrics of some song evaporate as they left my mouth.

I never saw the girl's breath coming out of her mouth. She only ever sat at the table in her warm kitchen or in her warm bedroom or her warm living room to study with a glass of warm white milk in front of her. Nobody ever asked her if she had her wool hat. I loved that question. I loved it so much. Now that's an important question.

If my mama didn't answer the phone, I would just stay in bed. Lying back, feet facing forward, knees slightly apart, hands on thighs, the TV on. I could lie completely still in that position for the entire day. And from there, finally resting, I would watch each TV show as it came on: the morning mass, the adverts, the midday news. Unrest, debt, hospital waiting times. On the other side of the glass door, too, a stream of silhouettes would pass by: the señor, the señora and the girl coming and going in the kitchen. And beyond that, the thrushes in the sky, a chincol pecking at the flower buds, the leaves on the branches shivering in the spring breeze. Outside, everything vibrated, while inside of me, silence was slowly sprcading.

I'd spend hours like that, in total stillness, waiting. Until, eventually, unreality would unpeel itself from reality like a shadow and I'd be able to see the air slowly enter and leave my chest, and the walls crack from some imperceptible tremor, and the wings of the tiuques overhead vibrate on contact with the wind, and the wind slip between the floorboards of my house in the south, and the south become as tangible as the empty feeling deep inside my body. Then, from somewhere far away, I would study these hands again: the burn marks on the backs, the hardened skin on the knuckles, the swollen joints. Two hands resting on a body that was dying, slowly but surely, from so much reality.

But you haven't locked me up in here for me to talk about my hands. About how even the touch of my own fingers against my legs unsettled me. About how I struggled to understand that those were *my* hands, that the air was entering and leaving the armour of *my* bones. It was a long time before I could get up. Only once night had fallen and the kitchen was empty and the darkness filtered through the frosted glass door would I sit on the edge of the bed and place my bare feet onto the floor tiles. With the cold rising up through my soles I would at last comprehend that it was me feeling that cold, and that reality was still there, ready to attack at any moment.

I'm begging you not to lose your patience. This is just the way life goes: a drop, a drop, a drop, a drop, and then we ask ourselves, bewildered, how we've ended up soaked to the bone.

I warned you from the start that this story has several beginnings: my arrival, my mama, my silence, Yany, and the dishwashing, ironing and fridge-stocking. But each of these beginnings necessarily leads to the same end. Like the silk threads of a spider's web, they all lead back to the centre.

On the night of 23 December I left the turkey soaking in tepid water. The señora bought a seven or eight kilo turkey each year, even though only the three of them would eat it. And since it didn't fit in the sink, I had to defrost it in the bath. The girl came into the bathroom, saw the turkey and asked if she could get into the bath with it. We all laughed: the señor, the señora, the girl. And me.

On the morning of the twenty-fourth, I pulled the turkey out of the tub and set about stuffing it with nuts and prunes soaked in honey. And while I was doing this, the señora came into the kitchen and, as if in passing, she said:

Estela, I've laid a place for you.

Sometimes her questions came out like that, coded as statements. She wanted to know if I would be having Christmas Eve dinner with them. Every year after that she would feel obliged to ask me this question, and all because, on that one occasion, the year my mama broke her leg, I shrugged my shoulders, earning myself a place next to them at the dining-room table.

I put on a grey skirt, a black blouse and some pink lipstick. I moved heavily, as if every one of those actions was a struggle, while in my head I repeated to myself: it's just another night, just another dinner, Estela, it's for your mama's leg.

When I entered the dining room and the girl saw me dressed up and wearing makeup, she pointed at me and said:

The nana's got clothes.

This time nobody laughed. We all pretended like we hadn't heard her.

The señor sat at the head of the table, the girl to his right, then the señora and then me, sufficiently close to the kitchen door.

The señor said:

Estela, some wine.

That was also a question. I had some wine. I served myself a slice of turkey and some duchess potatoes. Using the silverware reserved for special occasions, I cut up a small mouthful, placed it on a piece of plum and put it in my mouth. I chewed and swallowed, but I couldn't taste the turkey. So I gave it another go: meat, onion, plum, nuts. Again, I drew it to my mouth. But again, I couldn't taste it. I could pick out each of the individual ingredients I'd used – the butter, the pepper, the brandy, the oil, the honey, the gelatinous fat – but there was a gulf between each one. Because the parts have nothing to do with the whole. Because it wasn't just any old dinner. It wasn't any old night. It was reality again. Reality with its claws.

I was the only one who couldn't finish my food. The others left their plates on the table, empty and unmoving. I was slow – so very slow – to understand, but eventually I stood up, cleared the plates and then served up dessert for three.

What has the señora told you? Has she spoken about me? I'm sure she swore under oath that her maid was good-natured, reliable, humble, appreciative, quiet, that she seemed like a good woman. And when you asked her to talk about herself, she said: 'Mara López, lawyer', as if those three words provided a reliable definition. I'll define her for you, write this down:

For breakfast she ate half a grapefruit and a boiled egg, no salt.

She had a coffee as soon as she woke up, and was out of the house by eight.

She got home at six and ate a rice cake.

For dinner she ate rocket with seeds, chicory with seeds, spinach with seeds, cabbage with seeds.

Afterwards, in secret, she would eat a cheese roll polished off with a glass of wine and a handful of pills.

Ask her about the pills. I only ever saw the packages tossed in the rubbish bin week on week: Escitalopram, Clonazepam, Zolpidem. And then, once a month, the blister pack for her contraceptive pill. But who isn't on something? Even my mama was once prescribed some little pills. She went to the doctor about a pain in her chest. She said she had a hole as deep as a well inside her and that sometimes, at night, she couldn't take a deep breath. The doctor examined her, she coughed and he asked her a series of peculiar questions: whether she was happy or unhappy, if she was in debt or under strain, if she felt stressed or the cold made her feel depressed. My mama walked out of there with a prescription for tranquilizers and the well inside her only grew deeper and wider.

She was a good woman, the señora. I've told you that before. She treated me well, never raised her voice, and was a self-made woman who'd done everything required of her: she'd studied, got a degree, married, had a daughter. She worked hard, there's no question about that. She would come home tired and say:

I'm shattered, Estela.

As if tiredness were the surest proof of her success.

And she loved her daughter, of course she did. She adored her as you might adore a beautiful, fragile object. One that might break.

Be careful out in the sun, Julita.

Put sunblock on your ears.

Drink some water, go on, you'll get dehydrated.

When she first started refusing food, the señora didn't know what to do. She would just stare at the girl's full plate, then at Julia, and then back at the plate. But if I served the girl even the smallest scoop of ice-cream or bought her a sweetie with the shopping change, she'd drone on and on at me.

What have I told you, Estela? No sugar, under absolutely any circumstances. It's addictive, you know? Julia gets so full up on sweets that she won't eat her meals.

On other occasions the girl would prevent her from working. She'd crawl under her desk, cross her arms and legs and refuse to move for anyone or anything. It drove the señora mad. She would come into the kitchen and say:

Estela, you deal with it.

I'd make my way to the study and the girl would look at me full of hatred, although that hatred wasn't directed at me. She'd be rocking back and forth and compulsively gnawing away her fingernails. Did I already mention she'd bite them till they bled? More than once I saw her draw blood, and then she'd stare blankly at the red sores along the fingertips, as if they didn't belong to her.

Only once did I manage to get her out from under the desk, with a promise. I said:

Niña, if you come out, I'll plait your hair.

The girl looked at me and thought it over.

I want my mummy to do it, she said.

I promised and she came out, mistrusting but content. I went to the señora's bedroom and explained the situation. I'm not sure whether it was anger or regret that I saw in her eyes.

I don't know how, she said. You do it, I'm busy.

The girl cried herself to sleep.

In the evenings, after dinner, the señora would collapse into an armchair to reply to the emails she hadn't managed to get to during the day, or talk late into the night on her phone, giving all sorts of instructions: settlements, contracts, purchases and sales of land. It's true she worked a lot. She went above and beyond for that job. Dense forestation, squeeze the most out of the land, irrigate as little as possible, harvest at the right time. Did you know that they pull up the pine trees from their heads? That's what my mama used to say. Those poor pine trees never did anyone any harm. They wrench them out by their hair and the trees shriek, you can't imagine how they shriek. They pack them in so tightly on the land that they suffocate, grow to be weak and defenceless. Then they strip them of their bark, soak them in acid, cook them, grind them, and sell their mutilated remains. The rivers that irrigate them end up cursed, that's what my mama used to say. But now I really have branched off. For all the branches that are left.

Sometimes I would watch the señora eating. She'd serve herself a mountain of lettuce and devour it standing up in front of the TV in the kitchen: nationwide student protests, violent break-in at private residence, millions of pejerrey fish washed up on the southern coasts. She was worried about burglaries and violent crime. Then she'd say, anxiously:

Don't open the door to anyone, Estela. Under no circumstances should you open the door. They're robbing and setting fire to things. They're looting left, right and centre.

My worry, on the other hand, was my mama, so if the news mentioned the southern coasts I'd look up on the off chance that she'd appear on the screen in her rubber boots, with her new limp, with that well in her chest, collecting seaweed to go with the boiled potatoes. Meanwhile, the señora would raise one lettuce leaf after another to her lips, without ever getting the corners oily. Impeccable, in control. She'd make an elegant old lady one day. Trim, in a two-piece suit and with a single ring on her forefinger. An understated woman, that's the word. An understated woman with a diamond solitaire on her right hand. A stone intended to be passed down to her daughter, that exceptional girl who would grow into an exceptional young lady, then an exceptional woman, and eventually, my boss.

Children always choose which of their parents to take after. Think about your father, your mother, about the decision you made all those years ago.

And however much the señora denied it, that girl laughed like her father, spoke like her father and even looked at me the same way he did. Aged seven, she already brimmed with confidence.

I remember her third birthday. They celebrated it out in the garden, around a table with a big cake with meringue frosting in the centre. The guests were the señor's brother, his wife and two of the señora's colleagues. There weren't any other children there, did you know? Rarely were there other children in that house.

The señora came looking for me in the kitchen and said I must join them to sing 'Happy Birthday'. I didn't remember singing being part of the job description. That was a joke, relax. One of those jokes that help you get to the truth.

We all stood around the girl, apart from the señor, who was filming. He'll show you the video. None of the guests are in it, just the cake and the girl. You can hear singing, we sang. I'm singing in the video, too. You can make out my voice, slightly lower in pitch. That night, listening to it being played back over and again at dinner, I thought: Estela, that's your voice. And I couldn't believe it.

The girl turned three that day, did I already mention that? And aged just three, with that solemn expression on her face, she looks on each of us in turn. Watch it for yourselves. The expression on the face of that girl who all of a sudden looks eighty. That girl who would never age because her face, her infant face, already contained all of her future faces. Sometimes I think that's why she died. She'd used up all her future faces. But that's a ridiculous thought. Strike that out, please.

When she turned seven her father decided to teach her how to swim. This is an important event. Another of the story's beginnings that leads directly to the ending. He had the pool cleaned so that he personally could teach his daughter. So that under no circumstances would she ever drown.

She was still very small and she hated the water. I've already told you she cried every time I bathed her. When she was a baby I would take her in my arms, check the water temperature with my elbow and sing her a nursery rhyme to distract her. Useless. The moment her little feet went near the water she would start crying inconsolably. Once she was a little older, I learned to negotiate with her: an hour of cartoons, two hours of videogames. That way I could at least get her to take her clothes off, but her scowl only ever faded once she was dry.

I was in the kitchen preparing lunch. Slicing a tomato or soaking some lentils, who knows. Outside I heard splashing, so I went to take a look through the double doors in the dining room. The señor had dived into the water and was calling out to his daughter not to be a chicken. The señora was watching them from a sun lounger, fully dressed and wearing a straw hat. And the girl was debating which of them to go to.

She approached the edge of the water. The sun had made the flagstones around the pool so hot that the girl had to hop up and down on her scorched feet. She got as far as the steps, took hold of the rail and began to descend. Her body disappeared further with every step, and she was trembling. Really trembling. The señora called over from her lounger to leave the poor girl in peace, but I think by now you've got the measure of the señor.

Once the water was up to her waist, he stuck his arms out and pulled her in. The girl screamed and clung to his neck, but then, very quickly, she went quiet. They moved around in the water, jumping, smiling. I observed them from inside, exactly as you're all observing me now. I watched father and daughter, their happiness like a glass sphere encasing them.

In no time, the señor was able to hold his daughter by the waist as she floated on her front. She was a quick learner, the girl. She learned everything with great urgency. I noticed she was growing in confidence, starting to kick harder, her head just above the surface, her body supported by her father's hands. The señor was smiling and shouting:

More, more, more.

The girl was moving deftly, her kicking more assured. The señora sat up and removed her hat. The señor was still shouting:

That's it, that's it.

Then suddenly, he fell silent. The moment he let go of the girl and took a step back, he went silent and looked up over to his wife. That look of satisfaction. God, I hated that look.

The señora was frightened and she shot up and took two steps towards the pool. Even I was worried, and I went out into the garden. The girl was sinking heavily, her arms desperately flailing. The señor was close by, barely a metre away from his daughter. The señora started shouting, and maybe even I did too, I'm not sure. It all happened quite quickly. The girl, driven by some newfound strength, pushed her head up out of the water. Her body had understood. She made her own way to the edge, helped herself up onto her forearms, heaved her torso out, and turned around. They looked at each other for a second, father and daughter, triumphant.

The day after that lesson, I was sweeping the hallway when I heard another splash. And my first instinct? To run out into the garden. There, that should answer any suspicions. The maid raced outside in desperation, a sole thought in her head: that the girl, emboldened by the previous day's lesson, was drowning, choking on water, exhausted from her futile flapping, her fingernails blue, half-dead. When I reached the garden, I stopped in my tracks. Down at the deep end, the girl was holding on to the edge with her head poking out of the water. Standing over her, on the side of the pool, was the señor. And out of his mouth came one word:

Under.

Her head went under. Thousands of bubbles moved aside for her black hair, rolling and rippling in the water. Seconds later, the gasp for breath.

Again, the señor said.

And then:

I want to see you get out of the water without any help, without using the stairs.

This time, the girl went down much further, disappearing to the very bottom of the pool. She pushed herself up to the surface and tried to get out. She couldn't. She hadn't used all her strength.

Again, he said.

I don't know how many times she tried, but finally, using the very last of her strength, she managed to climb out of the water. She lay there on the edge of the pool, face down, upset. She had goosepimples from the cold. Her whole back was heaving from her coughing.

Very good, he said. Now get up.

The girl stood up.

Don't be afraid.

I didn't know what he was talking about. There was no reason for her to be afraid. The girl was out now. Out of danger, safely on the pool's edge.

Stay calm, the señor went on, although I'm not even sure he got the word 'calm' out before he pushed her in.

The girl fell backwards into the water. There was a loud, resonant splash. The señor didn't flinch. They looked so alike, father and daughter. Like two drops of water. He was rubbing his hands together. He did that whenever he argued with the señora, whenever the girl refused to eat or got a word wrong. And now he was rubbing his hands together because his daughter was taking too long. This time she hadn't had time to fill her lungs with air. Her body sank deeper and deeper, and from the bottom, the girl seemed to say in turn: 'Don't be afraid', 'Keep calm,' 'I'm going to count to three'. It was an endurance test.

The señor crouched down at the water's edge and I ran towards them. The girl's body was still sinking. He was about to jump in to save his daughter. His beautiful daughter. His fellow drop of water. But there was no need. The girl repositioned her arms and legs, found the bottom of the pool with the tips of her toes and propelled herself upwards. Once above the surface she took a deep breath, climbed out of the pool and stood up. Oh, how she coughed. Her eyes were red but her mouth was set in a satisfied smile. And she was about to burst out laughing when the señor pushed her in one last time.

I suppose I've gone on too long, wasted your time. You want me to talk about the death. I'm guessing that's what I'm here for. Very well, here goes, write this down on your notepads: The death can wait. Death's the only thing that really can wait in this life. First you need to know what I mean by reality, how it expanded as the weeks went on, how it took over my hours and my days until I could no longer escape it.

They decided to throw a party. I'm talking about New Year's Eve, the eve of the year the girl would die. A masquerade party with champagne and blaring music. Thirty guests, the señor said. Thirty-two counting them. Thirty-three with the girl. I suppose I was number thirty-four.

The señora approached the frosted glass door a week before the party and, without entering, without looking at me, began to do some sums. She was the only one who ever discussed money with me. Although discuss isn't the best word for it:

I transferred your pay, Estela.

Here's twenty thousand pesos for the vegetables.

Leave the change on the side table.

I included a little Christmas bonus.

I've mentioned before that they were good to me. Generous, transparent. And they trusted me.

The señora had used that word: trustworthy. They needed someone loyal. Presentable. An exceptional maid. I was supposed to be going back south for a visit, but I didn't make it that year either. I guess I was too proud to go; I didn't want my mama to see that she'd been right. I didn't want to have to admit that it was better in the south. With its leaky roofs. With its frosts. With its gossipy neighbours sniffing around outside your windows. You're a stubborn mule, my mama said when I announced to her that I was going to look for work in Santiago. And she was right.

I remember that the señor entered the kitchen just then, looking for something. He heard his wife talking about New Year's Eve and wanted to throw in his two cents' worth.

It's just another night, he said, only you'll earn triple pay.

And then, chuckling:

Even I'd consider it.

Even he would consider working as a housemaid on New Year's Eve. That's what he said, followed by a hollow laugh.

The guests started to arrive at around nine. Colleagues, relatives, people I'd never seen before. They rang the doorbell and filed in, dressed up and smelling of perfume. Little squeals of excitement. Questions that nobody would reply to. The girl was the only one in a mood, although that description doesn't do her state justice. She'd barely eaten a thing or slept for days. The noise was upsetting her, the people were irritating her, and she was afraid of the masks. The truth is she'd been like that for some time. I say 'that', but the right word will come to me.

I didn't throw her out when she came into the kitchen, or challenge her when she wanted to go into the back room. I never usually let her in, but as long as she sat still and watched the TV without bothering me, that night I didn't mind. She looked at me in puzzlement, then sat on the edge of the bed and turned on the TV, and the hours passed, as they tend to do. On the news they were showing New Year's celebrations in Beijing, Moscow, Paris, fireworks in London and Madrid. I could hear the clinking of glasses over the sound of the TV. The new year was approaching the world over; there'd be no stopping it.

The señora was driving me mad, constantly popping her head around the kitchen door with individual instructions, and speaking in an increasingly slurred voice:

Let's serve the canapes, Estela.

Let's put the champagne in the fridge.

Let's wash the wine glasses.

Let's clear the plates from the table.

By which she meant that I should serve the canapes, wash the wine glasses, chill the champagne and clear the plates, but without stacking them, without any clumsy accidents.

Time passed. An hour, a week, a whole life. I was to cook the lentils that would keep their pockets deep and wash the grapes that would bring them good luck. In the south, New Year's Eve was completely different. I would go down to the sea with the Jaimes, my cousin Sonia and my mama, and at midnight we'd watch the flares being set off from the boats – the fishermen praying, with that light, for substantial hake hauls in the year to come, for no bans on harvesting sea urchins, for no red tides. I think that's what I was doing, thinking about the south, when suddenly I heard the countdown. I went into the living room. The girl ran in as well and hugged her parents' legs.

Ten, nine.

They were shouting in time with the radio, at full volume.

Eight, seven.

They hugged, gathered in pairs or in threes, and held hands.

Six, five.

The señor, the señora and the girl, all together, smiling.

Three.

Two.

One.

Another year over, I thought.

They hugged and kissed. They wished one another success, love, money, good health. They appealed for work and wealth. They patted one another on the back and cheeks. They were excited, I saw them with my own eyes. Standing in the kitchen doorway, I watched them and, without meaning to, unable to stop myself, I started to smile. I smiled because that's what people are like. We smile and we yawn when the people around us smile and yawn.

The well wishes were followed by the kind of silence that falls when nobody knows what to do. Because absolutely nothing had changed. It was just another minute, another hour, the merciless passing of life. During this hiatus the señora looked up and directly at me. She came over cheerfully, put one arm around my shoulders and with the other handed me a glass of champagne.

My Estelita, Happy New Year, she said, and she kissed me on the cheek.

The señor followed her lead.

Here's to a good one, Estela.

And then, one by one, all of the guests:

A jolly good year to you, Estelita.

May all your wishes come true.

Easy on the champagne, it'll go to your head.

Wishing you love and happiness.

Good health and money.

Money and good fortune.

Thirty-two times they said it. And thirty-two times I said not a single word back. The señora didn't move from my side. Keeping her arm around me, smiling before her audience, she showed me off. And the smile on her face wasn't directed at the others, but at herself.

I don't know what happened next. I imagine they went back to their partying and I to the kitchen. I do remember, though, slipping into the back room and seeing that we were already ten minutes into the New Year.

They must have left at around four or five in the morning. And when the sun came up, after I'd mopped and dried, bleached and tidied, I collapsed onto the bed. On the other side of the frosted glass, beyond the kitchen, the sun was appearing from behind objects, revealing their outline.

I closed my eyes. A high-pitched beep was ringing in my ears. My temples were throbbing. I could feel a headache coming on. I felt a sudden sense of doubt. Just as I had on my first day, when I arrived at that house. Exactly the same feeling. I didn't know if that night had really happened, if all that had been real. I sat up on the edge of the bed and stared into the light filtering through the frosted glass. And a thought came to me then, a very strange thought, but one more real to me than having washed up and dried every single fork in the house, more real even than the feeling of my hands against the fabric of my uniform. It occurred to me that my life – that is, the life of the woman sitting on the bed – was somehow temporary. That's what I thought. As if I were in a film that sooner or later would end, and then there in front of me, immense and luminous, would be true reality.

Let me guess what the señora told you about the girl. Delicate and shy, beautiful, she loved her to pieces. Sweet, intelligent, a perfect child. A little picky, but brilliant, undoubtedly exceptional.

Generally speaking, the girl bothered me very little. She often spent the afternoon in her room, kneeling on her rug, surrounded by toys. Sometimes I got the feeling that she played as if it were something expected of her, as if she could feel her mother's disappointment at how taciturn and solitary a daughter she had turned out to be. What had brought such a sad creature into the world, I would think. I had to creep around her silence if ever I needed to interrupt her. And when I did, she would look up at me surprised, as if she'd forgotten who she was or who I was.

One afternoon she managed to get herself sent home early from school. Do you know this story? The teacher called the landline and told me that the girl was feeling unwell and that they were sending her home. It was a Thursday. I remember it well because she always had after-school activities: dance, French, karate, I lost count. She got off the school bus holding her stomach, the edges of her eyelids red, her eyes sunken. For a second I thought she really was sick so I bent over and put a hand to her forehead. Her eyes were shining wet but her skin seemed cool and not at all clammy. She waited until we were both through the front door and then start running around. She must have argued with a classmate, or got bored, who knows. She always did whatever it took to get what she wanted. Exactly like the señor, as I told you, and that day she celebrated her victory by bounding and shrieking all over the house.

I ignored her while I finished ironing the pile of clean white laundry. Sheets, towels, blouses, underpants. Once she could see that the laundry basket was empty, she persuaded me to go out into the garden with her. She was restless that afternoon. She wanted me to do her hair. She practiced doing forward rolls. She kicked a ball around. She skipped. Her impatience was giving her itchy feet. After a while, she had an idea. I was to lie on the ground, close my eyes and wait.

I told her absolutely not. I'd get my uniform dirty, I didn't have time for silly games. I still had to marinate the fish fillets, fry the garlic for the rice, scrub stain remover into a coat, and tidy and mop the floor in her room. But the girl played her usual card:

Just for a little bit. Go on. Is it so much to ask, Nana?

I lay down on the dirty ground, under the great vaulted ceiling of the fig tree. I'd never been there before. It was a new perspective: the inverse of a tree I thought I knew so well. The branches were groaning under the weight of their black swollen fruit, and the leaves quivered in the feeble breeze. The girl took off her shoes, knelt down beside me and tilted her chin down towards her chest. Then she brought her bent arms to her waist and clasped her hands together. As far as I could tell the game was to pretend it was a funeral. She began muttering some lines and swaying back and forth. And overhead, the branches of the fig tree swayed with her. I watched her for some time, unsure what my role in it all was, until suddenly, as if she were waking up, she opened her eyes and stood bolt upright. She gave me a wry smile; she'd had another idea.

I observed her pointy nose, her long, brittle neck, her sharp jawline. She'd grown thinner, I thought. And all that fragility reminded me of death. Her eyes, though, were still alive. Large, dark eyes that were scrutinising me.

I think she held me there for at least an hour. The sky grew steadily dimmer and my gaze was fixed up there among the black figs and the black leaves and amid an unfamiliar feeling of calm. Then I felt the girl's hands on me. Small hands mapping a rigorous course over my entire face. My forehead. My eyelids. The tip of my nose. I remember asking myself in that moment if I was happy. A serene, suffocating sort of happiness. Those hands stopped at the edge of my mouth. No, I wasn't happy.

In a grave voice, the girl said:

Open your mouth, Nana. And close your eyes.

I have no idea why, but I did as she said. I could feel my eyes sinking to the back of my forehead and I opened my mouth as if to let a falling fig land on my tongue. Just then the girl made a sudden motion and I felt my mouth, my whole mouth, fill up with a fat fistful of dirt.

The girl ran off around the garden, cackling. And I stood up, re-entered the house and locked myself in the back room bathroom. I rinsed out my mouth multiple times; sludgy, dusty mouthfuls. I wasn't angry, if that's what you want to know. I was more perturbed than angry. I think I was even a little afraid.

Once the water from my mouth ran clear, I changed my uniform, shook the dirt out of my hair and put it back up in a bun. And just then, from outside, I heard a scream.

The girl was limping but she didn't dare enter the house. Her parents would be home soon and she was afraid I would tell on her, that I'd tell her father that his daughter was a liar, that she'd feigned being ill just to get out of school early. I called her from the window and asked her what had happened. She didn't reply. I went out and took her by the armpits, as if she were a baby. She'd grown so much.

With enormous effort I picked her up, led her to the kitchen and sat her down on the worktop. She was barefoot and I noticed her little toe was completely misshapen. She was moaning and grunting. Not a pained noise: the girl was furious, flushed with hatred.

I went to get an ice cube, and when I returned I realised she'd been stung by a bee and that the stinger was still sticking out of her red, swollen skin. She was clenching her teeth. No sound but that stifled groan. I removed the stinger with my fingernails, placed it on the palm of my hand and showed it to her. She was still sunk in her rage, unreachable. With my free hand I rubbed the ice cube over her toe to numb the pain. Blowing on the sting, I said to the girl:

The bee's dead.

That caught her attention. She looked at me curiously. First at me, then at the sting. I told her that when that beautiful, noble insect – with its black head like a jewel and its torso wrapped in a fur coat – had pierced her with its stinger, it had ripped its own body apart. It had sliced its belly in two and died when it planted that sword into her toe.

Her big, deep eyes shone brighter than ever. I showed her the sting and said:

These are its remains. The sword and the remains.

I said that stinging her had been a punishment, but one felt by the bee itself. And that this sort of punishment is called a sacrifice.

The girl gulped. She looked at the bee sting and I knew exactly what she was thinking. She'd grown, it's true, and she was smart and strange, but I didn't think she had it in her.

I kissed her on the forehead and helped her hop down from the worktop. She was staring at her toe as if it were hiding some great mystery. I crouched down in front of her and, pre-empting her, I said:

Listen, niña. This isn't like a favour. You don't return sacrifices.

She smiled, but I knew she was no longer listening.

The backache started that night. From having picked up the not-so-little girl, from forgetting my own body. The señor, in his doctor's voice, prescribed painkillers. Three times a day, he said and he left them on the kitchen worktop. I took one, but the throbbing was still there, crushing my waist, pinching my legs.

When the señor and señora left for work and the girl for school I went into the master bedroom. She kept all sorts of pills in her nightstand drawer: muscle relaxers, Cipralex, Clonazepam, Zopiclone. I grabbed a few of each kind and slipped them into my apron pocket. For several hours I felt okay, the pain was manageable, but later on that afternoon, as I went to put a roasting tray of meat in the oven, I felt a sharp crick in my neck that ran all the way down to the soles of my feet. I took two pills at random, one light blue, the other white, and swallowed them.

As I cleaned the chopping board, a few grains of sand settled under my eyelids. I splashed my face with cold water and, without drying it, I waited. Droplets dripped from the tap into the sink, the leaves on the fig tree rustled in the wind, the blue flame cooked the meat. The pain had vanished. I touched my back and couldn't feel the pain or my hands. It was like being in a dream. Or not quite. It was like being dead, you know? That's what Señora Mara López – lawyer, forty-six years of age – must have done each night: die.

I lay down on the bed and thought about how there was nothing separating me from the objects around me: the sheets, the lamp, the damp stain laughing its head off on the wall. In the south, too, if I couldn't sleep, the room would start to go blurry. The blackness outside would slide in through the window and the land would devour the house with us inside it. Nature's indifference has always been a comfort to me: the way that, come night-time, we would cease to exist; the way the night went on without us. The same was true of things: the bed, the door, the nightstand, the ceiling. Things that had come before me. Things that would outlive me. And with that thought going around in my head, I closed my eyes and fell asleep.

The wait for dinner always drove the girl mad. I don't know exactly when it started, when she was three, or maybe four – a total aversion to food. She would scream, throw her toys, kick the walls. And not because she was hungry, by the way. She never had any trouble overcoming her hunger. Once she had her plate in front of her, she would push the pieces of chicken around in disgust, play with the sweetcorn, pick out the peas as calm as you like, one by one. The lead-up to mealtimes, on the other hand, drove her crazy, but that afternoon I ignored her. I didn't tell her to calm down. I didn't send her into the back garden to collect woodlice.

Maybe that's why she came into the room where she found me sleeping. She might have knocked on the door, a real little lady, and said:

Nana, I can see smoke.

Nana, I can smell a nasty smell.

Who knows how long she stood there at my bedside. I couldn't hear her voice. I could only hear the throbbing calling me back to reality. The girl was hitting me as hard as she could and a crippling pain was shooting up my spine, from my buttocks to my shoulders. Her clenched fist was punching me in the small of my back, just beneath my waist.

Nana.

Nana.

Nana.

Nana.

I could have slapped her, punched her, shaken her, screamed. I didn't though, don't worry. Instead, I turned around very carefully making sure not to snap my back in two and I told her, in a whisper, that we'd be eating later on, that I couldn't get up.

She glared at me and hit me even harder.

I told her she'd have to wait because I was in spasm.

Nothing, only more punches.

I explained that the pain was terrible, like when the bee had stung her.

The girl didn't react. Finally, I grabbed her hand, squeezed it hard and said:

Get out of here, you little shit!

Why should I have to explain myself to a spoilt brat?

Still spaced-out from the pills, half in the world of things, half returned to myself, I headed to the kitchen. It was full of smoke and smelled of charred meat. I took the roasting tray out of the oven and discovered I'd burned the food to a crisp. I salvaged one small serving, cut it up into little pieces and placed her plate of meat and rice on the kitchen table. The girl usually ate there during the week. The señor and señora ate later, in the dining room. I ate alone at the end of the day, once I'd done all the washing up.

As always, the TV was on in the kitchen. A very elderly lady was pointing at an area of parched land. Her animals had died: goats, horses. She was explaining that the waterway had been diverted further upriver. It's all dried up, she said. So there's no life here anymore, she said. At the table the girl licked her lips and drank her glass of water. She always did this before eating, and then she'd say: I'm full, I'm not hungry, Nana.

She sat in front of me with her feet on the seat and her knees bent up by her face. Only her eyes were visible from behind those knees. At this point our negotiations would begin.

Two spoonsfuls of rice, niña. You have to eat to grow big, or think, or live.

This time, however, she didn't move. Her arms were wrapped around her legs with her fingers tightly interlocked. I picked up the fork and was going to feed her as if she were a baby when, suddenly, she stood up, pushed her plate away to the very middle of the table and walked out of the kitchen. I didn't stop her. If she wanted to starve herself, that was her funeral.

The girl closed the door behind her and I listened as she pulled out one of the dining-room chairs. I heard her body settle into it and a little throat-clearing sound, identical to the one her mother always made before eating. The pain in my back was building again. I felt it creep all the way up to my ears, filling them. Then I heard the crackle of the girl's voice coming from the dining room:

Estela, bring me my food.

It was the first time the girl had ever uttered my name aloud. The *s* spoken with a drawl and the *t* like a hammer. Es-te-la. Exactly as the señora pronounced it. Exactly as the señor pronounced it. I don't know why it hurt so much to hear my name come out of her mouth. What did I expect? It was my name, after all.

I stood up and felt a nerve in my back spasm. I couldn't straighten up fully so I walked towards her hunched over. I picked up her plate and saw that my hand was shaking. Correction, that's not quite right. The details are vital. My entire body was shaking. The girl had sat down in her usual place at the dining table and she was waiting for her supper with a stiff, straight neck, exactly as the señora did. I approached her from the right side and put her plate down in front of her. And she ate. In the dining room of her house. Served by a woman who at any moment would die of pain.

Let's stop for today, please. My back's hurting in this seat. Put a full stop in your reports and let me get some sleep.

Some things can't be learned. They simply happen. Breathing. Swallowing. Coughing. We can't avoid them happening.

At four in the afternoon, every day, the girl would have her snack. Not at four thirty or five; at four o'clock on the dot I was to take a plate from the cupboard, a knife from the drawer, the butter and jam from the fridge and give her her toast and milk. Sometimes she'd eat half the bread, at others no more than a bite, which she'd hold in her mouth for some minutes and then spit back out onto the plate. She did drink the milk though. A glass of warm white milk. Then I'd wash the dishes, sweep up the crumbs and put the butter and jam back in the fridge.

She liked doing her homework while I did the ironing. Lips pursed, neck straight, elbows off the table. Bring your food to your mouth, not your mouth to your food. I would watch the girl open her workbook, brush the hair from her forehead and sit upright. She memorised new words by staring at the opposite side of the kitchen, where the nana stood ironing, pointing her finger ahead of her and repeating aloud.

Vertigo, vertigo, vertigo, vertigo.

One afternoon, having finished her handwriting and maths exercises, she told me she wanted to iron something. I told her she couldn't and I carried on ironing her pyjama bottoms. I wasn't angry at her, if that's what you're wondering. That thing with the dirt in the mouth was behind us, the punches on my back and the tantrums were behind us. Whenever possible, you've got to put these things behind you, that's what my mama used to say if Sonia took money from her purse or the local shopkeeper refused to let her buy on credit. The girl, in response to my no, started yelling. To iron, that's what the little lady of the house wanted.

I told her that the iron was hot and that the steam could burn her.

You barely reach the board, I said, taking a shirt from the pile.

She stood up, abandoned her schoolwork and began running around the kitchen. Impatience, once again, was giving her itchy feet. She ran here and there with her arms wide open, banging into whatever got in her way: her exercise books, the fruit bowl, the pile of freshly ironed clothes.

At some point her hand caught on the iron's cord. It was strange what happened next. The iron teetered on its base and it felt to me like the kitchen wobbled with it, as if to prevent the accident. It wasn't enough, of course. Reality dug its claws in. The iron began to fall towards the girl's bare arm.

I told you earlier. Yawning, blinking, coughing, swallowing – there are certain actions that can't be learned. The iron fell towards that arm but was intercepted by the palm of my hand. Tsssss. The sound was exactly like the one garlic makes when it hits the frying pan. Then, silence. At some point, amid the girl's screams and the burn, I had left that place. I was outside of reality, outside the kitchen, and from there, from a long way away, I watched the scorching hot iron brand its mark onto the palm of that other woman's hand.

The burn took several weeks to heal. The skin went from red to pale pink and then turned a soft, smooth white. Here it is, look at it. I'd tell you to touch it if you weren't so comfortable over there on your side of the wall. They're curious things, scars. Have you ever thought about it? Probably the softest parts of our skin. Maybe that's what we come out as when we're born, I hadn't thought of it before: an enormous scar anticipating all the scars to come.

You must be feeling quite irritated. It can't be easy being in your position. Spending hours and hours listening to stories that never shine any light on the ending. I'm sure behind my back you'll say I'm purposefully trying to mislead you, to buy time with a handful of irrelevant anecdotes. Stories about the señor, the señora and the girl before she died. If that's what you think then you're mistaken. I've got neither time to gain nor time to waste. What I'm going to tell you is as natural as water turning to steam, as the force of gravity, as natural as causes and their inevitable consequences.

I can't remember if I told you about the fig tree in the back garden, about its maimed stumps in autumn and its great big leaves in the summer. In August, when the wind danced through its branches, I could smell its sweet scent as it wafted over to me, the smell of the tree's future. And in February, when its branches were weighed down with black fruit, I often smelled the warm, heavy aroma of their decay. All the ages of a tree; a tree throughout the ages.

I was in the back room, not quite asleep or awake, when I heard a pitter-patter in the garden. It's raining, I thought.

I couldn't remember the last time it had rained in Santiago, and now the ground would soak up the raindrops, the riverbeds would flood, the brooks and streams would once again cascade down the mountainside's parched ravines. I remember that I stayed in bed, lulled by the incessant sound, aware that the clothes were drying on the line outside, that I'd have to rewash them, hang them out again at the crack of dawn so that I didn't fall behind with my daily tasks. None of this seemed to matter. I didn't want to get up. The pattering grew louder. The air became damp. The garden would be inundated with snails. The lilies would flower. Moss would grow around the roots of the plum tree. I closed my eyes and sighed. The sound grew even louder. I didn't know the rain could be so comforting.

The day dawned a short while after, and the sun emerged as fierce as ever. I got up and rushed to the laundry room window. I wanted to see the garden shining and clean, the raindrops dangling from the leaves.

Outside, the clothes were waving in the gentle, dry breeze. The garden wasn't damp; the grass was as dry as ever. It hadn't rained, but I'd heard those raindrops. The water's murmur had lulled me to sleep. It was then that I noticed the black shadow around the fig's trunk.

Again I thought it must have been the rain, a dark patch left by those showers, but then it clicked. All of the figs had fallen to the ground overnight. A shiver ran through me and a sinister sweet taste filled my mouth. My mama had warned me that the earth dries up from the inside, that the signs were always clear and the land didn't lie. When I was a little girl the rain used to be torrential. Northern skies clear, southern grey, rain is surely on the way, my mama used to say. But rain was becoming a thing of the past. The wetland was covered in cracks. Trees had died. Drought, she'd say, was all anyone was talking about. It's coming, Lita, we need to be prepared.

And in the middle of that thought, the señora's voice made me jump:

Have you seen, Estela?

Of course I'd seen. The fig tree was going to die because it had cast off its future.

The señora told me to clear up the ground. Otherwise, she said, all the sugar would stick to the floor. So I went out with a bucket, I collected the smashed figs, I swept up those sticky fruits and I cleaned. Of course I did. I cleaned until every last trace of death had disappeared.

The tree would never recover, it had found its cause. After a few months they cut it down. Some men carried off a sack of wood but they left the trunk flush with the ground. The girl often counted the rings on the stump. Fifty. Fifty-two. The number was never the same, but what did it matter? What's the difference between dying at forty, sixty or seven? Life, without fail, has a beginning, a middle and an end. Sooner or later, death comes knocking. It might be drought. A plague. The flu. A rock to the back of the head. First comes a warning, a scare, a false alarm. And the fig tree was the warning for that family. But then, death comes in threes, that's what my mama used to say: after one death, Lita, the other two won't be far behind.

You're all aware it's no easy thing to kill an animal. 'Kill', that's right, that accusatory word. I'm sure you must have all murdered at least one creature in your time. Out of fear maybe, or necessity. A fly perhaps. A fly buzzing in your ears, zooming from one to the other, driving you crazy in that room where you sit huddled together each day. Or a terrifying, potentially deadly spider. Or a bee, a horsefly, a mosquito, a fish.

The neighbour's children killed a stray cat not so long ago. They cornered it, stoned it and then dragged it by its tail out into the middle of the street. I was raking the front lawn when I saw them leave it there and hide bunched together behind a huge flowering ceibo. I didn't understand what they were waiting for – the cat was already dead – until I heard a car come up the road. The driver did slam on the brakes, you know. He tried to stop in time but couldn't, and the car's tyres ran right over that animal, crushing it.

To me it was like the blood and the ceibo's bright flowers had merged into one. The driver got out and clutched his head in his hands. The children, crouching hidden, were all holding in their laughter. All apart from one, the youngest, who wasn't smiling. He had seen the dead animal on the ground. He had seen the car crush that corpse. He had seen the man holding his head in his hands. He had seen the red of the flowers and the blood. At his tender age, that child now understood suffering. And as I raked the orange leaves, gathering them into piles and hoping the wind wouldn't force me to start all over again, I thought, that is how memories are made. Only that boy would remember the episode with the dead cat, and for the rest of his life he'd know what he was capable of.

The girl, for her part, would understand the cost of her silence. Sitting in the front garden, pretending to play with her dolls, she had watched the whole scene in secret: the stoning, the meowing, the car running over the cat, the hoots of laughter. The girl had comprehended death, even if you find that hard to believe.

Wednesdays were a half-day at school. Her classes finished at one and by two o'clock our lunchtime battle had begun.

There are starving children, I would tell her.

Children with no bread, no lunch ... you are so spoilt.

Not long after that, the señora would telephone to check how much her daughter had eaten.

She was thin, emaciated, well below the percentile for a healthy weight, the señor said when they got back from the paediatrician. But nothing and no one could convince her to eat a round meal. Milk, yes. Sometimes some cereal, a few raisins, a nibble of bread.

At exactly three o'clock every Wednesday, the doorbell would ring. On the dot, without fail, the private tutor would arrive, ask me to make her some tea and then would sit next to the girl at the dining table. She had just turned six when they began her tutoring. And aged six she would sit up straight and progress at a remarkable pace. She could already add, subtract, tell her odd numbers from her even numbers. I would overhear her repeating out loud: two, four, six, eight, ten. One, three, five, seven. Neptune, Venus, Earth, Mars.

She had just turned three when she sat the entrance exam for a private school. Did I tell you about this? They'd been arguing for months about the best place for their daughter. Finally, they selected an English-language school with painting and music classes, in case she turned out to be an artist. They both went with her on the day of the exam; the father, the mother and between them their pale girl with chewed-down nails. Half-way through the test the psychologist left the room and asked to speak with one of her guardians. The girl, their darling little girl, having successfully built a tower with the building blocks, having recited all the colours and shown she could count backwards, had thrown herself at her young desk mate and bitten her on the arm. There was blood and bruises. Inconsolable wailing. The girl had understood her parents' instructions only too well: if you want to come first you have keep the others back. The psychologist recommended therapy. A smaller school, she said. But in the end, thanks to a contact who put in a good word, the girl was accepted anyway.

At the start of their sessions, the private tutor would try to distract her. She'd ask the girl if she wanted to paint something with watercolours, or to tell her what she'd done on the weekend, or to play hopscotch out on the pavement or watch TV. She did it for the girl's own good. To stop her developing too fast, breaking away from the pack and racing to the top all alone. The girl, though, always wanted more. That way she'd win a medal to show her father each night:

Listen to what I learned, Daddy, look, look: 'archaic', 'glut', 'protozoa', 'parallelepiped'.

The tutor eventually advised the parents to end her sessions. It wasn't long ago, ask the señor. She called the house and told them that the girl was too advanced for her age. She didn't need extra support. She found the girl to be stressed, unhappy, it would be counterproductive to go on. Reluctantly, they agreed.

Very well, the señor said.

Then he paused for a moment, hesitated and before hanging up said:

Let's resume in March.

Then he corrected himself.

Or, better still, the last week of February. To warm up the engine ...

On the first Wednesday without tutoring the girl seemed different ... happy, maybe. She even forgot to pull her usual scene at lunchtime and devoured some bowtie pasta with vegetables. At precisely three o'clock the front doorbell went. I wasn't expecting anyone, but the girl looked straight at me, clearly distressed. Nobody had told me to expect visitors. It couldn't be the tutor. I'd heard the call about classes being suspended with my own ears. I told the girl to wait in the garden and spoke into the intercom.

Hello? I said.

And at the other end:

Piano.

That's what happened. I'm not making it up. The señor and señora had gone and bought her a piano. It seemed strange to me that they hadn't told me beforehand, so I called the señora.

It's fine, let them in, is what she said.

Two men installed the instrument as the girl looked on, astonished. A third man, tall and slim, with long hair and thick-rimmed glasses, spent more than an hour running his fingers up and down the black and white keys. Once satisfied, he asked if someone wanted to try it. I knew that 'someone' didn't include me.

The following day, while I was busy vacuuming the rugs and dusting the blinds, the telephone rang. It was the school nurse. She was calling to talk to one of the girl's guardians.

They're not in, I said. Would you like to leave a message for her parents?

She told me it was urgent; she'd already tried their mobile phones and someone needed to go to the school as soon as possible to take the girl to the doctor. 'Someone', she said, and this time it was me.

I changed out of my uniform and into my trousers and a T-shirt, brushed my hair and set off to catch the bus. The school was more than thirty minutes away and when I got there, I thought I'd got the wrong address. There were security guards at the front gate and a reception with an enormous metal detector. I had to leave my ID there. It must still be there, in case you need it. The girl's screams made me forget to take it with me. I could hear those screeches from reception and I ran over to her.

Her left forefinger was dark purple, the tip bent completely out of shape. I felt dizzy all of a sudden, and hot. It felt like my own finger had been deformed. My mouth started filling with a bitter liquid. I think the nurse realised I was about to pass out, so she quickly explained that it wasn't a serious break. She went on and on about the possible causes of the injury. No one could explain how it had happened. The girl had been in maths class, sitting on her own at the back, when she'd let out a scream.

The detailed explanation was pointless; I didn't need it. The girl had fractured her finger and it had been no accident. She'd broken it herself, her right hand crushing the left forefinger to pieces.

She stopped screaming the moment we left the nurse's office.

Stop that noise now or I'll tell on you.

That's how I confirmed what had happened. We took a

bus to the hospital. I chose there and not the doctor's clinic, knowing full well that the señor and señora would hit the roof. What was I thinking taking her on a bus with a broken finger? Didn't I remember there was cash at home for emergencies? How careless of me, how outrageous, unforgiveable.

We waited for three hours before she was seen. Three hours in which the girl sat in silence, examining her right hand. That's the one she stared at, you see what I mean? Her good hand. The hand capable of destroying any other part of her body.

The doctor said it would take three weeks for the finger to heal and she fitted the girl with a cast which prevented any movement in her wrist and injured finger. I saw the relief on the girl's face, and I admit I also let out a sigh. Three weeks with no piano. Three weeks in which she might just be happy.

Not even two of those three weeks had passed when, one evening, the señor called me into the dining room. They were eating a potato hotpot and I thought perhaps he wasn't enjoying it. Sometimes he didn't like the food I'd prepared and I'd have to cook him a steak, but that evening the food was fine. What he wanted was a pair of scissors.

The big ones from the garden, he said, and he waited for me to come back.

He told the girl to rest her arm on the table and then he cut the cast right up the middle, from her elbow to her fingers. The newly released hand gave off a vinegary smell, but her finger looked fine. Straight and no longer swollen.

Get me some cotton wool and alcohol, he said.

That order was for me. The girl's order was to move her fingers one by one, touch her thumb with her little finger, make a fist. The girl did as she was told. She was on the verge of tears.

Good, the señor said.

Good, good, he repeated.

Then he said that she just needed to strengthen her muscles, get back into shape as soon as possible, and he looked over to the corner of the room. The piano, luckily, would be the perfect exercise.

One afternoon around that time, just a regular afternoon, I went out to do the shopping.

Almonds

Chia seeds

Avocado

Salmon

I paid and put the receipt away, and when I stepped outside, there was Yany. I told you I'd tell you about Yany, although she wasn't called Yany at this point. There she was, sitting waiting outside the supermarket, sweeping the ground with her shaggy tail. I'd seen her several times before, next to the guy from the petrol station. She'd even followed me one afternoon to the door of the house. She became excited on seeing me, and I had to take a step back to prevent her from jumping right on top of me. I gave her a couple of pats on the head, walked around her and went to make my way home, but she followed me to the front door and then left without a sound.

I saw her from the kitchen window a couple of afternoons later. Have I told you about that window? It's quite striking. It starts at neck height and runs all the way up to the ceiling. From the street you can't see inside: why have the maid on display doing the washing, the ironing, or staring blankly at the TV screen. From inside, though, the maid can see the front garden and therefore keep an eye on the front gate. And Yany was there, sniffing around the recently bloomed geraniums. She was looking for a way in, sticking her nose between the bars. Finally she chose the corner bordering the neighbours' garden, checked that she could squeeze under the gate, and pushed her way in.

I was surprised she could slip so easily through the bars, but that creature was all skin and bones. She sniffed her way around the front garden as if trying to pick up my scent; nose to the ground, a way to get her bearings. Maybe that's why she didn't head towards the front door. She walked all the way around the exterior walls until she found the passage connecting the front garden to the laundry room.

When she spotted me in the kitchen, she wagged her tail happily. It's true I didn't stop her from coming in. That was my mistake. My mama told me that night:

No way, Lita, not pets. Don't even think about it.

I didn't listen to her, of course. I remember Yany's first visit well. There was something unreal about the dog's presence, as if she could only exist in the petrol station, splayed out on the floor next to the guy in overalls, and not there, in front of me. She didn't dare enter the kitchen but instead sat down in the middle of the laundry room.

Pardon the interruption, but I want to make something clear. I've always liked animals. Swallows, grey-hooded sierra finches, sea lions. Turkey vultures, chucao tapaculos, kodkods. But pets, my mama would say, domestic animals – no way. Having to feed and water them, wash them, deflea them and then clean up their fur balls, their shit, their mucky footprints on the living-room chairs. And all the while getting more and more attached, only for them to go and die under your roof. Or worse, Lita: you end up having to put them down once they're old, once they start peeing all over the place, once they become a nuisance.

I stared at the dog for a long time. Her head was too big for her body, her coat long, light brown and covered in ringworm. The fur on her chest was matted in muddy clumps. I guess it's true what my mama used to say, that in the world there are two types of animals: those that beg and those that don't. And that mutt in the laundry room, without begging, without giving in to her hunger and thirst, simply retraced her steps and left through the same gates she'd used to get in.

I didn't see her again for a few days after that, but thankfully she did come back. The girl was in school, the señor and señora were at work and I was sorting through the bag containing all the plastic shopping bags, when I heard the familiar sound of the dog's ribs against the walls of the house. Yany was coming. Once again she padded right into the laundry room that led into the kitchen, and this time she sat down in the doorway.

I watched her for a good while before approaching. Why had she followed me? Why was she looking at me with those eyes? What was she trying to tell me? Only after some time passed did I speak to her:

You just behave, do you hear, damn dog? Don't you dare get mud all over this kitchen.

She seemed to listen to me, or at least that's what I wanted to believe. She cocked her head to one side, then to the other, as if asking herself when this human would finally summon the courage to approach her. Finally, I did. I knelt down on the floor very close, perhaps too close, and I held out a hand for her to sniff, just like my mama used to do, that brief moment of surrender.

You dummy, I said. I'm not going to hit you.

Yany seemed to weigh up her options before summoning her courage and giving my hands a sniff. Sprightlier now, she licked the palm of my hand with her rough tongue. It tickled and I pulled it away.

Yuck, I said, but our pact had been made.

Crouched beside her, I checked the fur on her back and then each and every pad on her four paws. They were almost black, and hard from the tarmac and heat. She had a red ringworm spot on her right ear, the odd flea and one tick, which I tweezed out with my fingernails. She didn't once complain. She let herself be touched and inspected by my hands, these very hands. And when she understood that the ritual had come to an end, she stood up, delighted, and spun around like a whirlwind.

I decided I would feed her something, but I also wanted to treat her ringworm, so I went off and came back with some of the señora's cotton wool, some antiseptic from the first aid kit and a piece of bread, which I kept in my pocket. I rubbed her ears with the ointment and stroked her. If she was going to spend time with me, I would have to train her. She'd have to learn when to keep quiet, when to leave. Most important of all, she'd have to learn to control her hunger. Because hunger is a weakness, the worst possible kind.

As soon as I put my hand in my pocket, Yany's whole body tensed up.

Stay, I whispered, taking out the bread.

Not for dogs, I told her, placing it on the floor between us.

No ... no ... no, I said, slowly retreating.

I threatened her with my finger and in a growling voice. I told her four or five times not to move. But she didn't hold out for a second. The moment I was far enough away she launched at the bread and swallowed it in one great gulp.

It looked like the dog was writhing in pain. I noted her ribs sticking out of her coat, her scarred, sunken stomach.

That's no way to eat, I told her.

Stupid, disobedient dog.

You eat slowly, I told her.

You savour it.

I don't know if she understood me. I suppose not. She lapped up her water in a few licks and only when there wasn't a drop left in the bowl or a crumb left on the floor did she look up. There was a wild look in her eyes. She wanted more. She was demanding more than I had given her.

She stood up on all four paws and bared her sharp, filthy teeth at me. Damn dog. Ungrateful bitch. But what happened next was far worse. She let out a growl followed by a loud bark. I told her no.

No, you damn dog!

She barked again. Then again. And once more. The neighbours would hear her. They'd ask the señora the name of their new pet. And to make matters worse, both the señor and señora would be home any minute. Yany had to learn how to keep her mouth shut. She had to keep quiet.

No, I said, and I raised my hand.

Shh, I repeated. They're going to catch you, damn dog. Shut up if you want to eat again.

But Yany, who at that point wasn't called Yany, but damn dog, fucking dog, bad dog, pain in the arse – as she must have always been called, my Yany, my sweet pup – was barking like mad.

I made a fist with my right hand.

For the last time, I said, be quiet, you damn mongrel.

But she didn't know how to. She couldn't contain her untamed animal hunger.

She intuited the blow as soon as I raised my fist. And she left her eyes open as she received it, to the head. I hit her with all of my might. With all of my might I hit that brick wall of a skull. Yany let out the last trace of that bark and then finally fell quiet.

I knelt down at her side, in pain. My right hand was still clenched but now my fist, my arm, my whole body was trembling. She could have taken her revenge right then. Sunk her fangs into my neck. I don't know what I was thinking when I hit her. I don't know what I was thinking every time I let her in and gave her food. Every time I petted her. I only remember unclenching my fingers and seeing there, in the palm of my hand, four little blood stains. My nails had cut four nicks into my skin, and now they were bleeding.

I'm sorry, I said, and I felt ashamed of myself. I was blushing in front of a dog, in front of an animal.

Instinctively I held out my hand to her again. The same hand that had healed and fed her. The same hand that had punished her. The dog lowered her muzzle and licked it without hesitation. And I stroked her for a long time. That soft head, that sweet, swollen eye.

She didn't come back to the house and I admit, I missed her. I missed that animal's company and so I went out looking for her.

I was afraid I'd find her crushed under the wheels of a truck or infected with rabies, foaming at the mouth, her eyes popping out of their sockets. Or having been captured by the neighbour's kids and hanging upside down, dripping in honey, pecked at by vultures and tiuques and other horrible beasts. That image made my chest tighten, which is how I knew I loved her.

I've always imagined the deaths of the people I love. As a girl nothing was scarier to me than my mama dying and that's what I would think about at night: fires, shootings, hit-and-runs, accidents. I know it's lethal to think like that, but I can't help it. That's how I prepare myself, you see? By anticipating the pain.

When I left the supermarket with the señora's skimmed milk and rice cakes, I spotted the dog at the petrol station under the seat where the attendant always sat. I felt my body grow light and I hurried over, almost running, to greet her, but when she saw me she let out a low growl.

The young guy calmed her down and stroked one of her ears.

Easy, girl, that's what he said.

She smacked the floor with her tail and the petrol attendant smiled. His eyes smiled too. I remember it like a discovery: those small, narrow eyes smiled when he blinked. The dog jumped out from her hiding place and put her muzzle right up close to my apron pocket. I'd bought a bone to give her the next time she visited, but I it gave to her then, without a second thought. Maybe my mama was right: that's what people are like. I stroked her head, her warm, velvety ears. I let her lick my hand and then decided to head back.

I had already set off when the attendant called out and asked if the dog came to my house too. It seemed she was something of a scrounger, went from house to house, from one kitchen to the next. I nodded but also explained that it wasn't my house.

The guy smiled again. His gums were pink, like children's gums when they lose their milk teeth. I looked at his thick, chapped lips and noticed the uncurved edges, a straight line anticipating neither joy nor sadness.

Where you from?

Those were the words he used. The dog gazed at him as he spoke. She loved him, I thought in that moment. It was a look of adoration. He told me he was from Antofagasta, but he'd grown sick of mining.

Too much grind for too little bread, he said. No one ever sticks it out there.

Yany rolled over on her back while he drew figures of eight on her belly. I remember he seemed both young and old to me. His face young, his hands old; his voice young, his words old, that's what I thought. Or maybe I'm just thinking it now.

Do you smoke? he asked, offering me a cigarette. Behind him there was a No Smoking sign. I shook my head and we stood there in silence.

Shall I tell you a joke? he said suddenly.

My mama detested chatty people. She'd leave the bakery in a foul mood, her ears ringing with gossip about this or that neighbour, so and so's lover, the Jaimes' girlfriends. The baker swallowed a radio, she'd say, frowning. The guy from the petrol station talked nonstop, and the smoke from his cigarettes wrapped itself around his words, but it didn't bother me. Yany was still facing the other way, happily letting herself be stroked. He told me the joke. It was pretty funny. We both laughed and I listened to our cheerful snickers. If you want, I'll tell it to you. The joke I mean, maybe it's important.

Hey, boss, do I have to work on the Day of the Dead?

Why, you dead?

No!

So you'll work!

We laughed for a long time. When we fell silent, I told him I had to go, then crouched down and stroked the dog.

See you soon, he said, and I left.

When the intercom rang the next day I looked out the kitchen window and recognised the petrol guy's orange overalls. He was walking away as Yany, my Yany, slipped through the bars of the gate, loped around the edge of the house like before, and popped her head into the laundry room.

I always knew it was a bad idea. There was no way that story was going to end well, but I was just so happy to see her. I prepared her a bowl of milk, another of fresh water, and popped a piece of bread into my pocket.

Her head was poking through the doorway and she made as if to enter, but I told her No and she stayed put. She knew that order. On smelling the chicken casserole with rice I was making for lunch she grew desperate and let out a bark. I told her No again and gave her the bread. She understood, of course. She couldn't bark or come in, but she could come to the laundry room from time to time to receive a chunk of bread, a drop of milk and all the water she wanted.

From that day on she became a regular visitor to the house. Sometimes two afternoons a week, sometimes three. If the señor and señora were at home, I would flap my arms wildly and she would retreat, meek and uncomplaining. If I was on my own, though, I would let her stay in the laundry room and give her some food. Just a little, hardly anything, to make sure she never depended on me.

I don't know what I could have been thinking that whole time. I suppose I was hoping to keep the secret until the day

I left that house for good, and that she would come with me. What did you think? That the maid didn't dream about about leaving? That really would have been a perfect ending: the maid, her apron cast aside, running down the tree-lined street. And behind her the dog, the damn dog, tongue out, fur blowing in the wind.

That afternoon I was cleaning the floor, running the damp mop over the wood and then squeezing, squeezing, squeezing until the water came out clean. Yany was asleep in the laundry. Her skin twitched, driving off the flies that regularly landed on her back. The girl was in her room with a fever. Viral, according to the señor. She hadn't gone to school and she was forbidden to leave her bed. I was to make her lemon and honey, white rice with vegetables, and to keep checking her temperature. And she was to stay put in bed. That's what her father said, and her mother repeated. I saw my chance and took it.

I don't know what the girl came to the kitchen for, I only remember her reaction. The door to the laundry room was open and on the other side, there was Yany. Her already feverish eyes lit up even brighter.

Is she yours?

That's what she asked.

She wasn't mine, Yany. She wasn't anyone's. An animal like that would never belong to anyone, but I replied that she was.

Yes, I said.

And what's she called?

She was called dog. Damn dog. Fucking dog. Sometimes she was also called pooch, little pup, silly mutt.

But I was silent. I looked at the girl, then at the animal, then back at the girl. I'm not sure where the name came from. Naming is always a mistake.

She's called Yany, I said.

The girl said she was pretty, although in truth the dog was really quite ugly. Scrawny, scruffy, with decidedly unfriendly eyes. A charmless dog, but I'd grown fond of her and now the girl had discovered her and would tell her mother and father and they'd kick us out, first the dog and then me. I couldn't breathe. My chest was suddenly full of hot air. My hands and feet were tingling. The only thing that could calm me down was the sound of my own voice. I crouched down in front of the girl and looked her straight in the eyes.

It's a secret, I told her.

She nodded, gravely. She was an intelligent child, I've said it before.

She asked me in a whisper if she could touch the dog, and without waiting for my reply she tiptoed out into the laundry room, knelt down next to Yany and ran her hand over the space between her two ears. I exhaled all the air in my body. I knew, then, that she loved her too. The girl and I both loved Yany. And sometimes in life that's all you need.

The girl pretended she was still poorly and I covered for her that week. I told the señor and señora that her temperature hadn't dropped, that she'd vomited twice and was still out of sorts, the poor thing, and so we spent five days together, the three of us.

It was one of the few weeks that Yany visited almost every afternoon. The girl was happy. The dog was too. Everything would be okay as long as the girl didn't give away our secret. One night she nearly did, when she asked her parents if she could have a pet. A big, old dog with round eyes and a brown coat. The señora looked at her suspiciously, but just then the phone rang and she forgot all about it. How I hated the girl in that moment, and not only for her loose tongue. I hated how greedy she was. I hated her for wanting everything for herself.

Time passed, I'm not sure how much, but not enough. Happiness is always served in small doses. Write that down in your margins somewhere.

I've mentioned before that this story has several beginnings. It started the day I arrived at that house, but also every day I didn't leave. Although maybe the beginning wasn't my arrival at all, or the girl's birth, or the bee sting, but that first afternoon when Yany followed me and I made the mistake of letting her in.

I was in the laundry room, hanging out the clean sheets. Yany was watching me from the floor, half asleep, when suddenly she shot to her feet. I'd never seen her react quite like that. She took a couple of steps backwards and the fur on her back stood on end. She was a jumpy creature, so at first I didn't worry. She must have seen a cockroach or a spider or something. Maybe animals can have nightmares too. I was running behind that day. After I'd finished hanging out the sheets to dry, I still had to vacuum before the girl got home from school. And then there were the potted plants to water outside and the living-room rugs to beat and the rubbish to take out. Yany, though, was pointing her muzzle towards one corner of the laundry room, and that's when I saw it, against the wall, pulsating as only animals pulsate, humans included.

I've never been afraid of rats and I wasn't afraid that day either. It looked almost damp, its raggedy fur stuck to its skin, its tail bald and pinkish grey. As I say, I wasn't afraid, but I did recoil in disgust. The rat had appeared out of a gap in the wall and was creeping about in search of something or other.

I stood perfectly still and followed it with my gaze, but Yany couldn't help herself. She barked and bared her yellow, worn-down fangs. The rat froze, as if by staying still it could make itself invisible. It was just over a metre from where I was standing, and shaking uncontrollably. It didn't even stop trembling when it looked up at my face. Write this down, please, this seemingly unimportant detail. We looked at one another, the rat and I, and I was terror-stricken. A terror that rose up my legs and left me paralysed before that creature. Yany must have smelled my fear because she gave a great loud bark and at last the rat scurried back to its hiding place in the wall.

That was the first night I heard them. I was lying in bed, unable to sleep, when I heard a creak. At first I thought it must have been the wind, but outside there wasn't the slightest breeze. I heard it again, more clearly, and realised that the sound was coming from the crawl space above. They were up there, yes, there was no other explanation. It couldn't be just one rat. If you saw one, there'll be ten of them, Lita, my mama said, and of course she was right. Hundreds of miniscule feet scampering about overhead. A nest, I thought, and another shiver ran up my spine. A hidey-hole full of dirt and debris that they'd collected over weeks. A nest of fat rats with damp fur and wild eyes, that's what I imagined as I stared up at the ceiling.

I wasn't the only one to hear them. The next morning, when I took breakfast to the master bedroom, feeling haggard after a sleepless night, I asked the señor and señora if they'd heard anything out of the ordinary. They looked at one another, speechless, and nodded in unison.

How disgusting, the señor said, sitting up in bed.

He'd been hearing them gnawing away above their heads for several nights. The señora even thought she'd seen one out of the corner of her eye in the garden, but it hadn't been more than an inkling, a remote possibility.

My question had brought those rats to life. They were definitely out of control up there, and it wasn't long before the signs started to show: rat droppings in the larder and around the kitchen bins, suspicious noises coming from inside the wardrobes, darting shadows on the walls. There must have been a plague of rats reproducing above their heads, sneaking out in the middle of the night to devour the rotten leftovers in the bins. The señora said the key word:

Dangerous.

These were no cute house mice.

They're rats, she said. Rats infected with serious, contagious diseases.

Hantavirus, she exclaimed with wide eyes.

Her beautiful little girl infected, feverish, dead.

That afternoon the señor came into the kitchen carrying a cardboard box which he placed on the table. Printed on one side of the box was the image of a skull and in red the words: KEEP OUT OF REACH OF CHILDREN. Detailed instructions described how the substance acted on the nervous system, how long it would take for the rodents' vital organs to shutdown, the precise cause of death and the technology used to prevent the tissue from decomposing. Instead, the corpses would be desiccated: shells of dead rat. You wouldn't even have to clean up the remains. The suffering would be minimal.

A swift death, the señor said once he'd finished reading the description, and he slid the box across the tabletop and into my hands:

Take care of it, please.

That wasn't a favour either. The maid was to put on her yellow marigolds, break the security seal on the box and sink her fingers into those small blue granules. Blue, who knows why. Of all the possible colours, the poison was the colour of the sky, the exact same colour as the sea.

I told the señor not to worry, I'd get it done that afternoon. Then, the moment I was alone in the house, I opened the box, pressed the foot pedal on the bin and watched as the fine blue pellets fell to the bottom of the rubbish bag.

The mere idea of opening the attic door petrified me. And poking my head up into the heart of the nest was the stuff of nightmares. I could almost feel their claws scurrying up my arms, their tiny feet running down my back, all the way down to my own feet. No, absolutely no chance. I threw away half of the poison. Just enough proof to support my lie.

That evening, as the three of them ate dinner in the dining room, the señor wanted to know how it had gone with the poison. With a sinister glint in his eyes, he asked if I'd seen the nest and what it was like, how big, and if, in the darkness of the attic, the light in those animals' eyes had gone out. The girl looked at them in puzzlement. At her father. At her mother. Under their very roof. It was one of those stories made up of questions.

Were there lots of them, Estela?

Were they gross?

Did you see them die?

Sometimes just a nod is enough.

The strange thing is that I didn't hear them after that for some weeks. It was as if my lie had somehow killed them, or they'd gone and eaten the poison out of the bin. Or as if the house had never been infested in the first place. Maybe it had only ever been one rat and it was now wedged between the jaws of an alley cat somewhere. I stored the box of poison on the top shelf of a cupboard and forgot all about the rats. The family forgot about them too. It was a problem best forgotten.

Everything happened very quickly after that. So quickly you'll be on the edge of your seats. I'm talking to you, my friends, or whatever you want me to call you. Put an asterisk in your notes, mark what's coming next, because this is the point when the cards come tumbling down.

It happened like this. I'll grant you a little shortcut.

The girl was doing her Spanish homework at the kitchen table, tracing the big and small letters of the alphabet – A a, B b, C c – with exasperation. She could already read and write. Her father had taught her words like 'stethoscope' and 'penicillin'. She hated doing her homework and that afternoon she was groaning in boredom in front of her stack of exercise books. Meanwhile, the hot iron pressed her father's pants, her mother's gym tops, her cotton pyjamas. Yany was curled up on the floor of the laundry room.

After a while the girl reached her limit, closed her books and began doing circuits of the kitchen. I told her to go out and play in the garden, collect woodlice, skip up to 2,523. I told her to count her own steps, to draw some deep-sea animals, to hold her breath for as long as she could. If only she'd listened to me for once.

It was a Tuesday, did I already mention that? On Tuesdays and Thursdays the rubbish van came by, and it was best to take the bags out before six. By seven the communal bins would always be full and you'd have to press down everyone else's rubbish to make space. I hated touching those bags. Their suspicious warmth, the liquid oozing out from imperceptible holes and tears. It was better to get there early. To always be first. It must have been about four or five in the afternoon. There would still be plenty of room in the bins. I tied a knot in the black bag and told the girl to sit there quietly, I'd be back in a minute.

But when I walked out of the gate and over to the large dustbin, to my surprise it was full. The other women had got there before me. There wasn't a millimetre of space left. I looked around as if it was some sort of bad joke, but there they were, those black bags spilling over the sides of the bin.

I had no choice. Taking care not to touch anything obviously mushy or wet, I chose one corner and pressed down with one palm. I heard glass, cans and strange objects smashing, and then I felt a warm substance spreading across my open hand. I looked up towards the crown of a nearby plum tree as I pushed even harder. The sun was still up in the sky, filtering through the tree's branches and reddish leaves. Down below, the black bin bags and that black smell impregnating my fingers. With half of one arm inside the bin, I tossed the black bag into it and shut the lid.

The fetidness was hanging off me now. The smell of vinegar and mould and eggs and blood. I stood where I was, dazed, and lifted my face up to the sun. It was searingly hot. Barely a few seconds could have passed. But, then, who claims to understand the way time bends.

I went back into the house and to the kitchen. My eyes were blinded as I moved from the bright sunshine to the dark interior, and for a second all of the objects became wrapped in glowing halos. Only when I saw the girl did the light readjust. She was coming out of the back room, doubled over with laughter.

Correction. Scrap that.

The girl hadn't left the room yet. I saw the exact moment she put on one of my aprons. Monday's, Tuesday's – they were indistinguishable. I watched as her little arms burrowed their way up my sleeves and the checked fabric came to hang just below her knees. She stood there for a second in the threshold of the frosted glass door, but then she spotted me and said:

Who am I? Who am I?

I didn't know what to say. I was speechless. My hand was covered in rancid liquid; everything smelled of rot. The girl came bounding out of the room.

Who am I? Who am I?

She quickly grew bored. Making her way over to the larder, she opened the door, took out a kilo of flour and looked straight at me.

I have dough to make, niña, stop bothering me, she said. Keep still, niña. Settle down now. Go and skip to two thousand.

The girl opened the packet of flour and sprinkled its contents onto the worktop. Half of it fell on the floor, producing a white cloud that reached up to her knees. She walked straight over to the sink, filled a glass with water and tipped half of it onto the flour. A lumpy slop dripped down the sides of the counter. The girl then added the rest of the water to the mixture and a yellowish white puddle began to form at her feet. She stepped in it, covering the soles of her shoes before running off around the kitchen. There were sticky, stubborn footprints left all over the floor.

I'm sure you're wondering why I didn't stop her. Why I didn't shake her, shout at her and put her under the cold shower fully dressed. Listen to me carefully: my hand wreaked of mouldy rubbish; time had disappeared. The girl came back to the kitchen counter and managed to form a ball of dough out of the flour and water. She held it in one of her hands and walked towards me. The apron, my apron, was covered in creamy stains. My hand was still steeped in waste, the skin taut with grime. And the girl wiped her dirty hand on the front of my uniform, her dirty hand on the fabric over my heart.

Now listen to me carefully and put this on record. What I felt then was very specific. And so shocking even I was afraid. I didn't know it was possible to hate someone so purely.

I should have told her to stop, to put her clothes back on and to get down on her knees and clean the floor. To mop up every last one of those footprints with her tongue. To scrape away the encrusted flour between the floor tiles with her nails. I guess she could sense my anger. I could see her chest rising and falling, just like the body of that rat, just as alive, just as terror-stricken. I watched as she started to well up; at any minute she'd burst into tears. But I guess fear wasn't enough, or that at some point, looking at me, she noticed my hands. They were shaking, you see? My filthy, stinking hands, shaking uncontrollably. The girl must have remembered at that point who she was, and who I was.

She stared at me defiantly, picked up the flour mixture and, leaning back to gain momentum, threw it with all her might at the kitchen ceiling. The sound made both of us jump. First the hard thump, and then that unexpected stampede up in the crawl space.

There they were again. They hadn't gone anywhere.

The girl threw herself at me and flung her arms around my legs. I remained where I was, confused by the silence that followed. As if the rats were waiting for one false move as their cue to come down and launch their united attack. The girl was making soft, stifled whimpers. The rats had resumed their assault. Hundreds of them were racing terrified above us, startled by the thud that the girl had made at their feet.

And just then I heard a sound I'll never forget. At night, in here, it still haunts me. It was no longer the rats. This howl came from the laundry room. It was the cry of pain, of fear, that my Yany let out.

I looked through the doorway and saw Yany out there, her eyes wide open. I hadn't noticed her arrive that afternoon and she looked fine, in perfect health. I really didn't think anything had happened. And all I wanted was to wash my hands, slather them in soap, scrub my fingernails clean. But those eyes, oh, those shiny eyes of hers.

The girl was still standing behind my legs beside the door to the laundry room. I don't know what we were waiting for, either of us, but we both sensed something was about to happen and that we had no choice other than to wait for the inevitable. Like you might wait for the dawn.

Yany's top lip curled upwards and she bared her fangs at me.

No, I said firmly.

No. No. No.

She was a softy, Yany, I've told you that before. Docile, submissive, but we all have our limit. She had hers. I had mine. Even you people in there have a limit.

A string of saliva hung from one side of her mouth and I noticed her back go tense, preparing for the sudden movement to come. Yany shot up, ran and launched at me. And

I jumped out of the way. Or not quite. It was more like my body did the jumping, not me. And behind my body was the girl, dressed in my uniform.

It's strange the way some accidents happen. People often say they're over so fast there's no time to react. That wasn't the case here. A calm befell us, like in the clear eye of the storm: the dog, the girl, the rats, the rubbish bins. Yany opened her gaping maw and her fangs sank into that tight white calf. The girl didn't make a sound. She didn't react. Only once the dog had extracted her teeth did she scream in pain.

Yany recoiled in shock. Then she let out the saddest howl, as if she were saying sorry. As if she were begging me to forgive her for that brutal act. She ran into the laundry room, curled up in the corner and bowed her head. Only then did I notice the blood: Yany's hind leg was also bleeding. A rat had attacked her ankle. That horrible fat rat had dug its teeth into Yany's flesh. It must have heard the thud on the ceiling and lashed out. That's fear, don't forget: it makes us lash out. And this time the rat lashed out first; Yany only retaliated.

The dog's blood started to congeal in her dirty, sticky fur. The girl's, meanwhile, ran in two streams down her calf and onto the white lace trim of her sock. I looked at them both. The girl, pale. Yany, wearing a savage expression I'd never seen from her before.

I didn't hesitate for a second. I yelled at the dog. A harsh, loveless yell.

Out, you damn dog! Shoo. Go on, get out.

That's what I said. Go ahead and write it down. The words are important. Yany hobbled out of the laundry room, went around the house and left. Sometimes I think that this was the last time I saw her and that the dog who came by later was Yany's spectre, wanting to say goodbye.

The girl was shouting and sobbing inconsolably. Those two fangs had punctured her skin and nothing would calm her down. I took her in my arms, sat her on a chair and crouched down in front of her. I told her to calm down, that I'd get some alcohol and cotton wool. I couldn't make her better if she didn't stop crying. I wiped away the two trails of blood running down her leg. I pressed the cotton wool against the two small wounds for a few minutes. The girl was whimpering and staring at her leg almost in surprise. As if she'd only just realised that the wound belonged to her, that the pain, too, was hers, and nobody could ever feel it for her.

I disinfected her skin and whispered to her that she was very brave. That other little children would have cried much more. Others would have called for their mummies like babies. She didn't. She was a big girl, a special girl.

I managed to calm her down. The wound stopped bleeding. It wouldn't need stitches. I made a dressing using some cotton pads and a strip of sticky tape. I told her to stand up and take a few short steps. She didn't limp, her chest was puffed out. And as she walked along – imagining what she'd tell her school friends and how she'd leave her sock folded down to show off the wound like a medal – calmer now, almost proud, she took in the yellowish stain in the centre of the ceiling, the flour scattered all over the worktop, the sticky puddle on the floor, her filthy footprints and, finally, my apron. My uniform on her body and the bloodstain on the hem. A bloodstain that I would have to rub with salt and warm water. Then leave to soak. Then scrub by hand to get the blood out of the fibres.

The girl headed into the back room. I watched her take off the apron and put her school sweater back on. I watched her walk back into the kitchen, pick up a damp cloth and get down on her knees. I watched her clean, that's right. Scrub the hard encrusted flour while the cotton pad on her leg slowly turned red. The damage was already done, it's important you understand. Spilled blood can't return to its source. Just as a lifeless body will eventually sink underwater. Just as the crack that opened up that day would be impossible to mend. Maybe it was something about the sun or the rubbish. Maybe it was to do with the rat or Yany. Maybe it was me. All I know is that the girl was afraid I would tell on her, I was afraid she would blame me, and so we promised to say nothing. The girl and I. And no good can come of a secret. Write that down over there.

That night in bed I couldn't sleep for worry: the house infested with rats, the girl sick with rabies, yellow foam frothing from her mouth, her body in fits of spasms, the discovery of two suspicious white dots on her already pale white calf.

For days I looked after her leg as if it were my own. Alcohol, antiseptic, full-length trousers despite the heat. Luckily it didn't become infected. Her parents never discovered the wounds. And the hours dragged cruelly in Yany's absence. I was constantly looking out of the window to see if the dog was coming, but it was no use: she was never there.

One day I headed out to the supermarket to look for her. On my way I stopped by the petrol station where I found the guy filling up a sports car. Its bodywork sparkled in the sun, but the driver, from his seat, was badgering him to clean an alleged mark on the windscreen. 'There, there,' he repeated irately, tapping a spot on the glass in front of him with his forefinger. The attendant cleaned it but then took out a black cloth from his pocket and wiped grease all over the rear windscreen. The man drove off, furious.

Fucking lowlife. Scumbag. You've got a chip on your shoulder.

He accelerated and sped away.

The boy was wiping his hands with another cloth when he spotted me approaching. He smiled on seeing me, and I perked up as well.

Where's the pup? I asked.

You mean Daisy? he said.

No, no, no. She wasn't called Daisy. She couldn't be called Daisy. Names are too important.

The mutt, I replied, my mouth suddenly dry.

She'll be kicking about somewhere.

He shrugged and asked what my name was.

Estela, I replied.

I instantly regretted not lying. If Yany could be Daisy, I could have been Gladys or Ana, María or Rosa.

He was called Carlos. Charly, he added, flashing his small, perfectly white teeth.

Does Daisy still visit you?

I told him she did, but that she hadn't been over for several days. He promised he'd bring her to me.

I'll walk her over there, Estelita. As soon as she shows up I'll bring her to you. And he waved goodbye with his greasy black hand.

I was near the house when I spotted a bulky form on the ground at the foot of the communal bin. It's her, I thought in shock, and I felt a heat in my stomach. But it was just a bag, that's all, a large bin bag that someone had dumped beside the dustbin. I already knew I loved her. I didn't need to imagine her death, see her run over at a crossroads, poisoned in some forgotten corner, tortured by those spoiled cruel kids from next door. That vision terrified me. Most likely Yany had curled up on a street corner and died from an infection from the bite, alone, with no one stopping to help her.

When I reached the house, I shut myself away in the back room and decided to call my mama. She hadn't answered my calls for several days. Instead she sent me messages: I'm busy, I'm tired, let's talk on Sunday. I saw I'd missed a call from Sonia, but I didn't ring her back. Money, money, money, it was always the same story. I preferred my mama and her stories: never sad but happy, never cold but warm, never harsh, but gentle. I'd rather she told me about her afternoons spent combing the shore for mussels or the crabs caught up in the sea vegetables' tentacles, or about the treasures that the tide had washed up onto the beach. My mama, though, didn't pick up. I called again that night and, once again, there was no answer. I did start to worry then, yes, and the thoughts of death returned. My mama dead from a heart attack or a stroke. Electrocuted. Drowned. I didn't know what to do.

After hours spent lying awake, twisting and turning on the mattress, I finally pulled myself together. My mama was always leaving her phone somewhere: in the bathroom, between the pages of a magazine, in the cutlery drawer. It was normal for her not to answer. She must be busy working, that must be it. Her hands kneading dough, mashing potatoes, chopping firewood, sweeping soot, pointlessly pressing on with the repair of that wreck of a house.

And Yany must be skulking around some plaza in town, I said to myself in the darkness of that night.

And someone will have given her some water, that's right.

A young woman saw her and gave her a bowl of clean water.

And a piece of bread.

And she stroked her ears, yes.

And disinfected that peculiar wound on her hind paw.

And dressed it, that's right.

That's people for you, I repeated to myself before closing my eyes.

That's people for you. That's people for you.

And another day's work was done.

On several occasions I thought I heard Yany. Sometimes I was sure I could hear the little whimpers she would make when she napped, or I got the feeling that someone was watching me from a corner of the laundry. That uneasy feeling kept me on high alert. Or not quite. That's not it. The uneasy feeling came later; I think at this point I just missed her. The maid had grown fond of the street dog and the days dragged painfully without her company: cleaning the windows with window spray, polishing the brown shoes with brown polish, the black shoes with black polish, unblocking the sink, taking out the rubbish, replacing the bags, taking them out again.

The girl, over those days, ate without a fuss. Maybe she was afraid I would tell on her for staining my apron, for getting flour all over the floor. If I served her chicken, she ate the chicken. If I gave her salmon, she ate the salmon. She still took an hour to eat, and chewed each mouthful a hundred times, but her plate would be left sparkling.

I also stopped eating for a while when I was a girl. Did I tell you this story? Just for a couple of weeks, which is precisely how long I lasted at the girls' boarding school in

Ancud. My mama's employers at the big villa had asked her to move in and work as a live-in maid, and so she'd come to me and – never one to mince her words – said:

There's no one to look after you or cook for you. The boarding school's close to my work.

She dropped me at the entrance to the school one Sunday evening, and that same night I found I could no longer eat. There was nothing wrong with the food – lentils, beans, stews, chickpeas – but a lump in my throat prevented me from swallowing it.

The nuns didn't know what to do with me. I would take one bite of my morning hallulla bread and butter, and nothing for the rest of the day. They refused to call my mama, to involve her in the histrionics of a lazy, disobedient little madam, as the dining monitor put it when she saw my untouched plate. The Mother Superior tried to convince me that I'd soon get used to life there. The other girls weren't mean, and besides, my mama had to work, put food on the table, earn her living. She couldn't leave me alone out there on the land.

I don't remember if the girls were mean or not. I haven't held on to a single face, to a single name. You can forget what you don't name, we've been through that. I do remember a long, long hall and how, looking down from one end of it to the other, the dining monitor seemed very short, like one of us girls. I also remember the high ceilings in the communal dorm, the creak of the dusty stairs, the empty waste ground on the other side of the windows. I wanted to be gone from that place, to go back to the land with my mama.

I didn't plan it, I promise. It was a rainy lunchtime. I remember it well because on rainy days the huge windows in the dining hall would mist up and more than ever I'd feel I was going to be trapped in that place forever; there was nothing beyond it, no streets, no nature. It had all been swallowed up by the fog and the only thing left was the boarding school floating in a misty hellscape. I joined the line in front of the kitchen, was served a plate of charquicán stew and then looked around for the dining monitor. She was eating with the nuns up on a small wooden platform on the other side of the dining hall. I didn't even think about it. I walked over there, stopped directly in front of her and threw my food in her face. And with all my might, a strength I didn't know I had, I threw the empty plate at the back of the Mother Superior's head.

Don't work yourselves up, please. I told you: we all have a limit.

The Mother Superior fell to the floor, smashing her two front teeth. The dining monitor, meanwhile, still covered in potato and squash, grabbed me by the wrist and with her other hand slapped both of my cheeks. For some reason the canings that followed didn't hurt. It was as if I were no longer inside my own body, as if I'd already left that place.

That afternoon my mama came to collect me, and from the school she led me straight back to the land. There doesn't seem much point in telling you about the silent journey from Ancud back to our house. She didn't look at me the whole time, nor once we arrived. That night she cooked potatoes and pork chops, which I demolished.

You silly ass, she said, while I sucked the bones.

When my plate was clean, she looked at me and dissolved into laughter. At first it was more of a snicker, as if she couldn't hold it in, as if her mouth had been taken over by that laugh, but it grew louder and louder until she was doubled over.

A whole plate of charquicán in her face! she cried, with her head thrown back and her shoulders shaking uncontrollably. I sat there, frozen to the spot. My mama was really in hysterics now: open-mouthed, her eyes creased, tears running down the sides of her face. The laughter was catching and soon the pair of us could hardly breathe, two belly laughs in the infinite blackness of the open countryside. Eventually she grew tired and we both stopped laughing. Her face went back to normal; the edges of her mouth turned down. She said, very seriously:

Everything has consequences, Lita. You must understand that.

The next day, she woke me at daybreak and told me she was going back to her job as a live-in maid. I was thirteen years old, soon to be fourteen, and I stayed there, out on the land, on my own. Or not exactly on my own. I had the pigs, the kodkods, and the neighbour's blind horse for company. And every morning there I'd be, battling against the wind to get to the bus stop in time for the bus that would take me to school, and with no mother around to tell me: Put your hat on, Lita. What did I knit you that wool hat for?

Little rascal, my mama said just before leaving the house.

And then, like a premonition:

You're going to have to learn to look after yourself.

The rats went back to their hideaway in the crawl space, the girl forgot about the dog, the bite on her calf healed well, and the señora moved up in her company. She was now the one in charge of getting all the title deeds in order for new pine plantations. The wood business was booming; they'd be opening a new branch in the south. She and the señor were discussing whether her pay rise would allow them to buy the beach house, or whether it was better to invest, maximise their revenues.

In the summer my mama and I used to go blackberrying. This isn't another digression, don't worry. The blackberries are important. She taught me how to pick them without getting pricked, how to avoid the thorns. It's all in the eyes, she'd say. You mustn't get ahead of yourself, because if you're already looking at the next blackberry, then – bam! – those thorns will get you. But they were always snagging on my clothes, my arms and hair. I never could control my eyes, which were always already onto the next blackberry, envisioning its sweet black dye in my mouth, leaving my slow hand behind to get caught in the knotty shrub. Once, I grabbed an entire bramble and put the whole thing in my basket.

What's that? my mama asked when she saw the still-green fruit.

You've been greedy, she said. Blackberries don't all ripen at the same time, precisely to prevent people from stripping the bush bare. We take today's fruit and someone else will take tomorrow's. If you take the whole bramble, others are left with nothing, Lita.

The green blackberries never ripened. They went rotten and I threw them away. The others, the black ones, we ate well into winter: blackberry jam, blackberry cake, blackberry kuchen, blackberry milk. But I'm rambling again, or should I say brambling ...

The señor and señora were celebrating her promotion with a bottle of champagne out on the terrace – her glass emptied, his untouched. I took them some paper serviettes and a bowl of olives. The señora took one and popped it in her mouth. As she ate, she would always brush any specks from her shirt. Even when there wasn't a crumb on her she'd still make sweeping motions with the back of her hand, wiping away those intolerable imperfections. On this occasion I remember her saying 'Cheers', drinking from her glass and then brushing off the dirt that was to come. That's what I thought, at least. Or perhaps it's just what I think now. That she was anticipating the dirt in which she'd soon be covered.

The girl wanted to try a sip of champagne. I didn't see if they gave her any. I went back to the kitchen to heat up dinner and that was when I heard the señora say:

Ju, I've got a present for you.

She had a present for her beautiful girl so that she, too, would learn the importance of rising through the ranks. So that her daughter would remember that climbing the ladder reaped rich rewards. I went out to ask the señor if he would be wanting rice. He was on a diet and often left his rice untouched on his plate, telling me:

Estela, I've told you not to serve me any rice.

But if I didn't serve him any rice, he would ask me for a little bit, a spoonful, or say, Do you want me to starve to death?

I was about to ask about the rice when the girl began opening her present. A fairly big cardboard box wrapped in pink and white paper. For a split second I thought that it must be a pet, and I despised her. She was going to have her own dog. A Labrador or an Old English Sheepdog. A German Shepherd or a Chihuahua. A hyperactive, destructive little puppy, an animal that wasn't my Yany, that would never be my Yany.

She opened the box, ripping the paper to shreds. The ribbons fell to the ground and were left there. As she studied the dress in her hands her face gradually turned a darker shade of red. A white dress with a lace frill on the sleeves and a pink sash to tie around the waist. You know the dress I'm talking about. The dress from the end.

It's for your birthday, the señora said. So that you can dress up like a princess at a lovely fancy-dress party.

It was weeks until her birthday, but there was the dress.

The girl looked at it, then at her mother and then back at the dress. How to describe that expression of hers? The look of desperation permanently etched onto that child's face.

A similar scene had taken place when she was younger. The señor had bought a pair of pearl earrings for his cherished little girl. A pair of perfect white pearls to adorn her perfect white face. The girl must have been four, maybe even younger. She didn't ever wear earrings, because they irritated her ears, but there were those pearls, inside a tiny blue box. The señor opened it and showed them to her and she recoiled in horror. He didn't even notice. He was too busy taking them out of their velvety case. Next he crouched down and with those pearls pierced each of the grown-over holes in her ears. The girl moaned and began to cry. The señor told her she looked beautiful, like a little señorita, he exclaimed, but most likely she didn't hear him. She was beside herself, kicking and screaming on the ground. And he, the señor, only fell quiet and stopped lavishing praise on his daughter once he saw what she was capable of. The girl then picked herself up off the floor, glared at him red-faced, wild with rage, put her left hand to her left ear, her right to her right, grabbed both pearls and yanked them almost to the point of ripping them from her earlobes.

I remember the heavy silence that fell between the señor and señora. A tight, tense silence. He ran to get some alcohol to disinfect his daughter's ears. Then he asked me to bring some ice and sterile strips to prevent the wounds from fully splitting open. The señora observed the scene as if it wasn't really happening. Standing there in shock, she looked at the girl as if she hardly knew her. Or worse: as if she were afraid she knew her too well. I stood there watching them all, unsure what to do. The girl was screaming and groaning, half afraid, half in pain. At that moment, the señor looked up at me. It was a look of pure malice. Because the maid had felt pity towards his family.

I don't know if they talked about it afterwards. Whether that night, in their bed, they whispered to one another about it not being normal behaviour. Whether they discussed the unmanageable nature of their perfect little girl. The one who refused to eat. The one who bit her nails. The one who hit her classmates. The girl never brought it up, I do remember that. She spent several days at home with a dressing on each ear, but the wound soon healed, erasing all memory of that episode from her skin.

And now, back in the garden, the girl was wearing that very same look of desperation as she stood holding her new dress, red-faced, inaccessible.

The señora took it off her.

It doesn't matter. It's not important, she said, clearly upset.

Then the señora turned and looked at me. Her maid, prime witness to her unhappiness. And no one likes their happiness to be called into doubt.

I don't know how many days passed, and I should know. Those were the last days of reality as I knew it.

The doorbell rang while I was in the middle of the ironing. So many hours spent ironing: folding every item in turn, pressing the heat into them. I looked up and my first thought was that it must be the postman. But then I remembered Carlos and Yany, and I went to answer the door. I know that at no point did I put down the señora's blue blouse. As if I were still ironing as I walked through the kitchen, across the hallway and outside to the front gate, where I was met with a face that didn't belong there: my cousin Sonia was standing with a rucksack slung over her shoulder and a brown envelope in her hands. It was summertime, and the sun shimmered in her hair but cast other parts of her into shade.

She didn't even say hello. She spoke as if those words had been burning her tongue and finally she could spit them out.

She's dead, she said.

The sun was still playing with her hair, making it white, like shining light.

My cousin Sonia spoke again:

She was working at the salmon farm when she just collapsed sideways like a sack of potatoes. She died on the spot, Estela, five days ago.

I noticed that a few sweat beads had merged together on her top lip and the corners of her mouth were turned upwards, like the mouth of a happy person. Now that mouth was telling me that she didn't know exactly what had happened. My mama had been gutting the salmon, descaling them, pulling out their eggs, when suddenly …

That's what she said:

When suddenly …

The words kept tumbling from her mouth, while up above the sun wrung more sweat from her brow. I patted my pocket, took out my phone and called my mama's number. On the screen the words: Calling Mama.

She would answer, of course she would. She'd say: 'Mi Lita' and dive into a story about the bottlenose dolphins splashing through the sea's surface or the black-necked swans floating at the water's edge. I wanted to hold on to those images: the swans' perplexed expressions, the black arc of their necks. The dial tone rang off: no answer.

Sonia explained that she herself had only found out the day before. My mama had been with one of her co-workers, some guy called Mauro. And don't be angry, she said, but I was in Punta Arena working at the crab plant processing crabs. Everything's got so expensive, so hard, Estela, there's not even enough money for firewood.

My mama used to say that spider crabs were actually spiders from Mars and that in the summer they'd be washed to shore, turn dumb in the heat and not even realise they were getting cooked there on the sand, slowly turning from grey to red, with each passing minute a little closer to a dollop of mayonnaise and a squeeze of lemon.

Sonia couldn't keep still. She kept shifting her weight from one foot to the other and moving the brown envelope from one hand to the other. She was wearing a brand new pair of trainers. I clocked them – she knew I had – and after that she didn't dare look me in the eye.

I had been sending her money each month to take care of my mama. To make sure she wasn't left alone out on the land, and that her leg didn't get any worse. But my mama hadn't even been at home. She'd been slicing open salmon bellies. She'd been pulling eggs from their guts, and those guts would then be fed to other animals that soon enough would also be dead.

Sonia started garbling something about how it'd been urgent, how you had to do these things straight away, and that Mauro, the stranger who'd worked beside her at the salmon farm, had taken care of it. I didn't understand what she meant. Her white shoelaces, the pristine seams on those trainers, the upturned corners of her mouth, the sun burning her cheeks, the sweat beads balancing on her brow.

He took care of the funeral, she said, and that was the last thing I could listen to.

That day, while my mama was being buried among the gnarled roots of a mañio tree, I had cooked a beef stew, swept the whole house and washed and dressed the girl. You expect to feel certain things: a sudden cool breeze on an otherwise hot day maybe, or like you suddenly hear the sound of your mother's voice. I'm talking about a hunch, a sixth sense. I've heard it called a presentiment. What a word, presentiment. But what is the feeling that comes before pain? For me that was the saddest part of all: that whole day I'd felt absolutely nothing.

Sonia looked down and told me she had to go. She'd come to Santiago to look for work because when she'd found out about my mama she'd left Punta Arenas to return to Chiloé and was fired.

She asked if I knew of any jobs going.

Anything at all, she said.

I'm broke, she said.

I don't know what I replied. I only know that as she was leaving she handed me the brown envelope and I slammed the gate shut behind her without saying goodbye.

I stood looking at the house in a daze. My cousin was outside. I was heading inside. And down in the south, my dead mama. I'd never know if that man had washed her and brushed her hair. I'd never know if he'd chosen her lace dress, crossed her hands over her chest, sung to her.

I think I took a couple of steps forwards, and then it happened. The front garden started expanding all around me. The spikes on the cacti came towards me, leaned in and then, just before they could spike me, they transformed into the branches of ulmos and monkey puzzle trees and winter's bark. The sun, too, swelled, and reality, the whole of reality, dilated to absorb all that brightness. The house, the stones, the crowns of the trees all seemed about to burst. Then, for a moment, every object around me shone, pouring with light, and I shone among them, a little less alone.

I returned to the house, but I'm not convinced it was still the same house. The objects inside were identical, as was the arrangement of the furniture. And yet I was somewhere else entirely. I went back to the ironing, either out of habit or because I was still holding that blue blouse with its blue creases. I remember blinking heavily, conscious of the rise and fall of my eyelids, while one thought whirred in my head: I would have closed my mama's eyelids and placed a button on her tongue before sealing her lips. All of her clothes were missing the top button because my mama used to pull at the neck of her apron or top – of whatever it was that was strangling her – to stop herself from suffocating. All of her clothes were missing the top button.

It was a good while before I felt reality digging its claws back into me. I was still alive. My chest was rising and falling. I was thirsty, hungry even. It couldn't be happening. I was supposed to return to the south after just a year working in Santiago. I was supposed to save some money to fix the zinc roof, build a front porch, add another room to the house and for us to live and die there, her and I, mother and daughter. And now I was supposed to go on alone.

I don't know how many hours went by. I only know that it grew dark and I didn't hear the señor coming in from work. I hadn't turned on the lights. I hadn't prepared dinner. I hadn't laid the table or even finished the ironing. The señor walked into the kitchen, flicked the switch and a bright white light made everything around me solid again.

What's wrong? he said, gruffly.

I merely looked at him, but it was enough for him to understand that something bad had happened. He came over, placed one hand on my shoulder and said:

I'm sorry, Estela. You'll feel better soon, don't worry.

I felt that heat again in the pit of my stomach, right here.

It's always annoyed me that other people think they know more than I do, especially about me. What did he know about my pain?

I put the blouse down on the ironing board. I know it was her petrol blue blouse because it was the only thing I ironed that whole day. Over and again, front and back. I would find it in the bin the next day.

I flinched, shrugging off the weight of the señor's hand, and tried to picture my mama's face. Her prominent cheekbones, her small eyes, the brown freckles on her forehead, her thin, arched eyebrows and square, slightly yellow teeth. I pulled the cuffs of the blouse taut and carried on pressing the fabric down and out towards the edges.

I wanted him to leave, but he didn't move. He wasn't finished yet. I felt sure he was going to tell me how sorry he was. He'd tell me all about the life cycle and how we're born, grow up, reproduce and die. He'd begin with the line, 'Listen, Estela, let me explain something to you.' And he'd explain something to me. Then he'd hand me a few banknotes for the funeral. I could almost see him rummaging around in his wallet, looking for the right amount: not too much, not too little. A seemly amount, enough for a woman like me.

None of that happened. Instead, standing there beside me, looking at me intently, he put both hands on my shoulders, leaned in and hugged me.

I fell silent. My mind, too, fell silent and an unbearable burning sensation appeared in my mouth and behind my eyes.

No, no. This couldn't be called a life.

It hit me later, when the sun came up and I sat on the edge of the bed with a horrible feeling in my stomach. I grew anxious and thought: Something terrible is about to happen. Then I remembered my cousin Sonia, my mama buried in the ground, and I could picture the rain hammering down onto the freshly dug mound of earth at the cemetery. It had already happened, you see. That terrible thing, that horrifying thing already belonged to the past. And I was still there on that bed, in that room, in that house. I was alive in that reality, carrying on without her.

By the time I went into the kitchen the señora was already waiting for me with a cup of tea.

Estela, dearest.

She'd never called me dearest. She told me to take a seat and handed me a wad of folded banknotes.

Head down south, she said.

And then:

It's important to be with family at times like these.

I looked at the money in my hands and ran through the journey in my mind:

The bus stop, blocks away.

Two buses to the metro.

The metro to the bus station.

The long queue at the ticket office.

Fourteen hours with my forehead pressed against the bus window.

The ferry crossing over the channel.

A colectivo.

A ten-minute trudge through the mud.

Knocking on the door, knocking on the door and no one answering it.

Thanks, I replied to the señora. I think I'll wait.

She advised me to take the day off.

Rest, Estela. It's important to rest.

It was important to rest. It was important to be with family.

I returned to the back room, slid the door closed and remembered the brown paper envelope that Sonia had left with me. Sitting down on the edge of the bed, I carefully opened the flap and shook it upside down over the mattress.

My mama's two hands fell out.

She pulled those leather gloves out every winter. She could be wearing a pair of ripped jeans and a worn old jacket, but she'd still have those elegant black gloves on. My grandma had given them to her to protect her from the cold. Because wool got wet. Because her hands would get chapped. It had been a gift to her daughter just before she died. I arranged the gloves on the bedspread, one beside the other. Her ten fingers pointing at me, as if she were sitting right there, the tips of her fingers grazing my own.

Have you ever noticed how hands get passed down from father to son, from mother to daughter? Look at yours if you don't believe me. Look at your nails, your cuticles, the shape of your knuckles. It might not be obvious at first. Young hands never look like those of the mother. But as the years pass, the resemblance becomes undeniable. The fingers expand. The tips grow bent. Age spots appear identical to the ones that were once on the grandmother's hands, and then on the mother's adored hands. By the time I was fifteen my hands were as big as my mama's. If I placed my palm against hers, our nails came to the same length. Her fingers thick and leathery, gnarled from all the work they'd seen, veins bulging under her skin, the backs all lumpy, and my own soft hands, still unblemished. I looked at my hands, then at her gloves, and I thought: the mother dies and leaves her hands in the hands of the daughter.

I put the left glove on first, then the right. They fitted me perfectly, not a wrinkle on the back, no gaping on the palm. I lay down on the bed and placed her hands on my chest. And that was when I remembered the fig tree. Its black fruit on the ground. That had been the warning: death always comes in threes. My mama was the first of the trio. There were two more to come. And I wanted to be next.

My silence began after my mama's death. It wasn't deliberate. It wasn't a punishment either. If I had to define it, I'd say it was more like a maze: after a while spent inside it, I could no longer find the way out.

I was frying a tortilla when the señora came into the kitchen.

Estela, she said, where are the matches?

And I passed her the matches.

Let's have chicken casserole.

And I cooked chicken casserole.

Julia's sheets need changing.

And I put fresh sheets on the girl's bed.

One afternoon a sock appeared on the kitchen table. Next to it, the sewing kit. Inside the sewing kit, a needle and thread. I threaded the needle, darned the hole and put the sock back in its drawer. Who needs words?

Yany no longer came to keep me company, I didn't have a mother I could call, and that opened up a silence in me so profound that anything anyone said was mere noise. I stopped answering the phone. I stopped replying to the señora. I stopped humming tunes while I polished the furniture. I stopped speaking to the girl. Not a single line, not one measly statement.

I don't know how long my silence lasted. And I use 'silence' perfectly aware that it's not entirely accurate but that it'll be easier for you understand that way. You can write in your notes: 'Claims to have kept silent'. Or ask the señora: 'Did your maid fall silent?' To which the señora will reply: 'I don't recall any silence.' Because I doubt a woman like her would ever recognise a silence like mine.

You might never have given it any thought, but words have a specific order. Cause–outcome. Beginning–ending. You can't just arrange them any old way. When we speak, each word has to stand apart from the one before, like children lined up at the classroom door. From small to big, short to tall – the words go in a particular order. With silence, on the other hand, all words exist at once: gentle and harsh, warm and cold.

I began to notice a few changes, although I'm certain no one else did. The quieter I was, the more commanding my presence, the harder my edges and the more telling my facial gestures. A few weeks went by like this. Write down in your documents 'several weeks' or 'an indeterminate number of weeks'; I've told you it's not easy putting events from that time in order. I didn't speak, I just did. Or I didn't do, and my not doing was a different kind of speech: not wiping the skirting boards, not dusting, not putting the chlorine in the pool and watching the water turn a darker and darker shade of green.

I also learned that there aren't words for everything in this world. And I'm not talking about matters of life and death. I'm not talking about lines like 'there are no words for some pain'. My pain did have words, but as I scoured the bottom of the toilet bowl, as I scrubbed the mould from the bathtub, as I sliced an onion, I no longer thought with words. The thread connecting words to objects had snapped and all that was left was the world itself. A world stripped of words.

But now I really have gone off on a tangent. Cross out that whole page, and the one before. You probably want to know if I killed the girl, or at least if I was the one who planted the idea in her mind. Underline this with a red pen: the girl drowned. She drowned, and yet, she knew how to swim. Ask the señor, ask the señora; she could swim like a pro. So explain to me how both statements can be correct; how there can be a reality in which both facts are true. Go on, make a defence for words. You over there, striking out whole paragraphs, hiding behind that mirrored window.

It was around then that things, objects, started talking for me. There was no above or below. No before or after. Without words, time can't even begin, you see? And it's almost impossible to tell a story without a beginning. The boiling water was my clock, fire was fire even if I didn't name it, and the dust still traced the outlines of the objects around the house.

Actually, no. You're not going to understand like this. I'll try another way.

With each day that passed, the silence embedded itself deeper in my throat and my words set hard. I became full of ideas and new questions. Like whether when things lost their names, they transformed in the same way they did when being named. Saying the words boss, master, mistress, manager, owner. Saying maid, nana, servant, nurse. Or refusing to say those things. You know? Those are also transformations.

And unconsciously, unintentionally, I trained myself. I think I only really understand it now; only now can I make sense of all the time I spent watching that stranger sweep the floor, discard the mouldy plums, wash the dustbin, clean the windows, remove all the hairs from the bathroom. I trained myself like sportspeople are trained to tolerate pain, like you and I have been trained to despise each other. And in training myself, I also trained her.

The woman who did the ironing.

The woman who watered the plants.

The woman who made the chicken casserole.

The woman who scrubbed the skid marks from the toilet bowl.

And pulled the hairs out of the drain.

And hot-pressed the trousers and underpants and her own uniform.

And scrubbed the mirrors wearing her giant yellow gloves.

And was taken aback by her reflection: the pinched face, the dry skin, the eyes bloodshot from all the bleach.

That woman who knew how to become indispensable.

Who learned how to plait the girl's hair.

Who learned to take down the doctor's messages.

To say not 'armpit' but 'underarm'.

Not 'they was' but 'they were'.

To put the knives in the knife drawer.

The spoons in the spoon drawer.

And her words in her throat, where they should remain.

Not speaking was easy for me. Yany no longer came by, my phone no longer rang, and my mama's voice, all her questions, had ceased to exist. My employers almost never asked me any questions. Or, at least, not the sort of questions that require a response.

That was actually the second time I'd lost my voice, although 'lost' isn't really the right word for it. Back when I was at the boarding school, and before the episode with the plate of charquicán, I caught pneumonia after not eating, after not feeding myself properly. That's what the Mother Superior said when she heard the whistle in my chest: You must eat, María Estela, you must feed yourself properly. Sometimes I think I made myself sick on purpose. I'd have rather died than stay locked up in that hellhole listening to the Mother Superior call me María Estela every morning.

The first thing I felt was a twitch in my back, followed by a sudden wave of tiredness. Then, out of nowhere, I found I could no longer get my voice out.

A spoiled brat, very stubborn, a little madam, the dining monitor said, and even though I was running a fever, she wouldn't let me stay in bed.

I didn't reply. I could barely breathe. My head felt heavy and my ribs were burning. My fever spiked. I grew pale. I was getting worse. Eventually they gave in and called for my mama. She waited for me downstairs in her own checked uniform. She saw me and was about to give me an earful for causing trouble, for not leaving her in peace, but instead, having placed her hand against my forehead, she took me straight to the big villa where she worked from dawn to dusk.

Go and see for yourselves: the house where she worked, I mean, not my dead mother. A villa set across several floors and directly facing the sea. Before we entered, my mama asked me to behave myself, and for God's sake not to cause a scene.

She took me to a small room leading off from the kitchen. A single bed, a nightstand, a chest of drawers. You know the sort of room I mean. She put me into bed and held a cool damp flannel against my forehead. Then I noticed a girl spying on us from the doorway. She must have been about seven or eight, several years younger than me, and she was wearing a pink dress with her hair in a long French plait. A plait braided by my mama, lock by lock.

Her parents owned a restaurant, did I mention that already? It was called El Porvenir. That's right, a restaurant called The Future. Sometimes my mama would have to clean there on the weekend, and she'd say, glumly: On Sunday I have to go and clean The Future. And I'd start laughing and a second later she'd crack up too. But I've digressed again. How is The Future relevant ...? My mama took off my jumper and covered me in a dry towel.

You're drenched, she said, and the mere touch of fabric against my skin hurt me.

After that she rubbed my chest with a menthol ointment and balanced the stub of a lit candle right in the middle of my sternum. The flame rose and fell and I watched it stand tall then sink back down, as if the sun rose and set with every breath. The smell of smoke and mint soothed me.

Just then her boss appeared at the door. She must have said:

What are you doing, you peasant? You'll burn her alive.

Or maybe it was just a look of irritation or revulsion at the sight of me smeared in that menthol ointment. The woman came in, took the candle off my chest and handed me two pills and a glass of water.

On an empty stomach, she ordered, and with that she left the room.

My mama didn't say a word in her presence, but I heard her silence as a kind of scream. Lying there, I didn't say anything either. What was I going to say? But when the woman left, I spat out the two pills and my mama, on seeing them half dissolved in my hand, kissed me on the forehead and smiled at me.

I woke up the next day feeling better, and my voice had come back. I asked my mama if I could stay with her in that house, play with that girl, live with those parents, eat that food. She was blunt, my mama. A woman of few words.

Damn kid, she said, and off we went, back to the boarding school.

Sometimes I ask myself what I would have said if I had spoken up and whether by doing that, by speaking, I might have averted the tragedy. I'm sure you all think so. You must be the kind of people who put a lot of faith in words. You think it's better to let it all out, sit down and pick apart the differences: the difference between the union and the leadership, between employees and employers, between that other girl and me.

I surrendered, voiceless, and eventually lost the desire to talk. With whom? For what? Yany had gone, and my mama was no longer alive. And the routine, over and again: taking out other people's rubbish, vacuuming other people's rugs, cleaning other people's mirrors, scrubbing other people's clothes.

Have you ever put your hands inside the dirty laundry basket? Have you ever sunk your fingers into that tangle of arms and legs that piles up in there? Every Friday I would empty my employers' laundry basket only to find their bodies mounted up again: brown stains in his pants, white stains in her knickers and sweaty black socks. I swear that sometimes, on opening the lid, I thought I heard their moans.

To avoid making two trips to the laundry room, I would bundle all the clothes in my arms and hold their intertwined, sour-smelling, dirt-encrusted bodies against my chest. And I would walk like that, carrying the señor, the señora and the girl, before letting them go on top of the washing machine and starting the process of separation: the señora's torso to the left, her breasts to the right, her legs to the left, feet to the right. Whites and colours separate. Synthetics and cotton separate.

A piece of clothing can hold a lot of secrets, I don't know if you've ever thought about it. The worn-away knees from repeatedly falling over, the shiny crotch from two chunky thighs rubbing together, the elbows threadbare from hours and hours of boredom. Fabrics don't lie, they can't pretend: where they fray, where they tear, where they stain over time. There are many more ways to talk. The voice is just the simplest.

But now I really have gone off track. Sometimes I wonder what you can all be thinking, whether you write down everything I say or are just waiting for the part you want to hear. Waiting for me to tell you, for instance, that my employers were good to me. That they paid me on time each month. That I preferred to be kept busy: raking the leaves, making jam, more and more things to speed up the course of my life. Or perhaps you're eagerly awaiting another story: the one about a maid who went to work in the villa when she was fifteen, who fell in love with the eldest son who used to pull her hair and tickle her. That's a sad story, for sure. Because one day that boy grows up and he backs the maid into a corner of the kitchen and sticks his tongue in her mouth. Or because one night he goes up to the attic where she sleeps, creeps through the door, slides his fingers between her legs and pushes his way in, breaking her in two.

Nothing like that ever happened to me. In Chiloé I worked in a supermarket, at a sausage-packing plant and selling newspapers on a street corner. Only later, when I was thirty-three, did I decide to try my luck in Santiago. But we've migrated south again; I still can't seem to keep my words on the right track.

I was alone in the kitchen cleaning the fridge compartments – the egg holder, the door shelf for the milk, the vegetable drawer – when I heard a hissing sound. It went like this: psst, psst, and then nothing. I ignored it but it came back: psst, psst, psst, psst. It was coming from outside.

I stopped what I was doing and looked out of the window facing the front entrance. Behind the gate, in his overalls, Carlos was waving, and at his feet, Yany, sitting calmly on her hind legs.

I could feel my eyes open wide and my heart start to beat faster. The dog was sweeping the ground with her tail and Carlos was on tiptoes trying to peep inside the house.

I thought I must be seeing things, that it was the ghost of Yany, but the dog that I'd believed to be dead was looking at me through the entrance gate with her sweet, almond eyes. I instantly thought of my mama. Perhaps she, too, would appear on the other side of the gate, as alive as Yany, or as a phantom. That thought saddened me but only momentarily. As soon as he saw me, Carlos nudged the dog, encouraging her to pass through the bars of the gate. And without hesitation, she obeyed him.

Here she is, Carlos said.

And then:

She always comes back.

He smiled at me and I smiled back at him. I remember it well because it felt like a gesture being performed by someone else's face. But that other face was smiling because the dog had returned. The little mutt stepped into the garden with her now healed paw and ran towards me.

I went out to meet her and she jumped right on top of me. And I stroked her dirty head and matted coat for a long time. After that, as if no time at all had passed, Yany lay down in the doorway and kept me company. And when the girl was due to arrive home, she left without a fuss. I wasn't going to make the same mistake twice. I wouldn't tell the girl she was back.

Shoo, I said in the afternoon, and she slunk away through the gate.

Sometimes I think Yany's return brought on the ending, and that those days with her were the final omen.

I don't know if I'd already begun to suspect this possibility. I was putting away the clean tableware from the night before – the cups with the cups, the plates with the plates – when I felt eyes on the back of my neck. It would have been about six thirty in the morning, the sun still hadn't risen from behind the mountain and the señor had just arrived home from the clinic. He seldom worked the night shift, but there he was standing in the kitchen, legs slightly apart, arms dangling at his sides, his white coat unbuttoned and his face fixed in a grimace.

He shuffled half asleep to the larder and took out a bottle of whisky. He wasn't a drinker; I've already told you that. It was the whisky reserved for guests. There wasn't much left in the bottle, but it wasn't exactly the hour to start drinking. He should have been going to sleep and waking up at noon, complaining about how tired he was, and about his patients, the heat and the food on his plate, but instead he collapsed into the chair and poured himself what would be the first of many glasses.

My shift finished at two, he said.

I wasn't even sure he was talking to me. He almost never spoke to me. An order, an instruction, but never a statement like that.

Four hours had passed since 2 a.m. Outside, some parrots were squawking away like an alarm, but he carried on talking regardless, like one of those people who are used to others hearing them out.

He'd never done it before, that's what he said. He'd never even thought about it, but when he spotted her in the street it was as if he were no longer himself.

I wanted him to stop talking. In half an hour the girl would wake up and I still hadn't had my breakfast or finished putting the glasses back with the glasses, the mugs with the mugs.

He said it had been an ordinary day but that as he drove home he'd been overcome with a feeling of boredom. A deadly boredom, were the words he used. And then he'd spotted that woman standing on the street corner and, without thinking, he'd pulled over.

I was holding a clean, dry plate. A plate that, had I dropped it, would have smashed on the kitchen floor, waking the señora and the girl, and changing the course of history.

If he could go back in time he'd drive right on by, the señor continued, but the woman opened the door and greeted him with disconcerting familiarity. He wondered if perhaps he knew her; she might be a patient of his. But he didn't recognise her face. She then told him that she knew somewhere discreet, and she told him where to park and which room to ask for.

I was frozen to the spot, as trapped by his story as you are by mine, only I was holding a clean plate in my hand, which I was supposed to be putting away. A plate that suddenly felt heavy. So heavy that my fingers couldn't bear it, couldn't take that weight much longer, and soon, very soon, would drop it.

The señor had stood at the foot of that hotel bed not knowing what to do, what to say to that woman, how to touch her or make a move, and maybe that's why his eyes were drawn to the sole picture hanging on the wall.

A photo of a desert, he said. A sun-cracked desert.

I don't know why he felt it important to mention that photo. What did the cracks in the desert have to do with that woman, or his boredom, or what was about to happen? The señor refilled his whisky glass, clutched his head with one hand and with the other used his forefinger to stir the amber liquid. I'd never seen him like that: his skin was ashen, his eyes bloodshot with purplish dark circles. Eyes that looked as though they'd started to decompose, I thought. As if the rot had already set in.

He told me that the woman had lay down face up on the bed, feigning an expertise she didn't have.

I sat next to her, he told me, and I slid my hand up her leg and under her skirt.

I kept wondering why this man was telling his story to me, to the housemaid he barely ever spoke to, and I thought about butting right in and telling him: That's enough. But my silence had already embedded itself in my throat and he carried on as if it was no longer in his power to stop.

She wasn't wearing any knickers. Those were the good doctor's words. Visibly uncomfortable, she let him touch her, although only for a moment. Then she closed her legs and told him he had to pay her first.

I realised that I couldn't stop him. Him or the story. I wouldn't be able to unhear what that man was about to tell me. And I, or rather my silence, was only encouraging him. As if each unuttered word of mine opened the way for another of his.

He asked her how much, precisely how much he should pay her, and the woman answered: Everything, pay me everything. She said something else after that. The señor thought he heard a gravelly, clipped voice, a voice full of loathing, giving an instruction: to take a scalpel, stick it in his cheek, and rip out his tongue.

Looking at him now in the kitchen, I could see that the señor didn't have a hole in his cheek; his tongue was still firmly in his mouth, but his face looked as if it might peel away from his head and onto the table. From there I would have to pick it up and put it away in a drawer: the tablecloths with the tablecloths, the knives with the knives, the faces with the faces.

Sitting on the edge of the hotel bed, the señor fell silent. Or at least that's what he told me. But it was a different kind of silence from mine. He told me he could feel the hole in his cheek, his numb tongue and dry mouth, and that he handed her all the money in his wallet. The girl looked at it, then spoke:

You and I will never see each other again, she told him. In twenty or thirty years you'll doubt this ever happened, that I really existed, that you sat down on this bed and emptied out your wallet. Now tell me your secret, go on. And I'll keep it for you.

I was staring at the señor and all I wanted was for him to stop talking. I wanted him to go to bed, fall asleep and wake up as he had on countless other mornings and go jogging and eat his breakfast and contemplate his own unhappiness in the mirror.

He must have noticed I was desperate because he looked at me strangely then, his still eyes tired and red, but inquisitive, as if he were seeing me for the first time. I'd lived in that house for seven years, and that morning, as the sun rose from behind the mountain, the señor looked up and he couldn't take his eyes off me. I stared back at him, wondering if I would be made to pay for having been witness to his weakness. And what the price would be. Just how high.

He said he'd been twenty-four years old.

At first I didn't know what he was talking about. Then I realised he meant that his secret had taken place twenty years ago, and now his maid would have to hear it. That's what he paid her for. A discreet, mute servant. As silent as the grave.

He had been just a month away from graduating and his supervisor had entrusted him with a difficult case, a fragile patient requiring sound judgement. He headed to the relevant room, past rows and rows of metal camp beds, and found his patient in one corner at the end, dying.

I can't remember her name. That's what the señor said, holding the palm of his hand to his forehead as if trying to pull his face back up over his cheekbones.

He approached the bed and for a second he thought it was empty.

She was that thin, he said.

That small.

At the foot of the bed were her notes, which he took his time reading. He assessed whether she needed any other medicine and worked out her age: seven years old. He loathed these cases. He'd never been able to understand paediatricians. Only at that point did he look up at his patient.

Her face was so pale you could see the capillaries under her skin.

He used that word, the señor. He used the word 'capillaries' and rubbed the floppy skin of his earlobes with the pads of his fingers, as if that way he could somehow touch the skin of the little girl in his memory.

She was dead, he told me.

There was nothing to be done.

He served himself another whisky and I noticed that the bottle was trembling in his hands. In mine, the plate was beginning to slip as my hands sweated.

The woman from the hotel ran her hand up his thigh.

It's over now, she told him as she reached his trouser zip.

She opened it, touched him and said:

I'll keep it now, okay? I'll keep your secret.

The señor spoke again:

When it was over, I closed my zip and stood up.

I noticed his speech was slurred from the whisky and I just wanted him to be quiet. I wanted to let that plate smash on the floor and watch the shards of porcelain shoot across the kitchen.

He never told me the end of the story. The doctor, I mean. The señor, the family man. I don't know if he told it to the woman from the hotel. I don't know if he went and told the senior doctor on duty that the girl was already dead, that there was nothing he could do. Nor did I understand why he'd kept it a secret. Downing his whisky in one, he stood up and said:

Sometimes I dream about that little girl. Sometimes I see her in Julia's black eyes. In Julia's paleness. In my own daughter's despair.

He refilled his glass for the last time, and then he asked me:

What do you see?

The señor stared at me with that face that looked like it was about to peel away from his skull and he asked me what I saw. What did his maid see in her employer's distorted face? He'd asked the woman from the hotel the same question. After telling her his secret, he asked her what she saw. And she answered in a fake husky voice:

I see a sensual man.

He stopped her, grabbed her roughly by the arm and asked her to tell him the truth. She paused, then looked him coldly in the eyes and said:

I see an empty shell.

And she was entirely right.

The woman fell silent after that. The señor told me he could see fear in her eyes. I know fear only too well, he said to her, adding that he wouldn't lay a finger on her.

He lay down on the bed, suddenly dizzy. It felt as if the hotel walls were caving in. The air was now thick with the rancid smell of that old hospital. The woman asked him what was wrong. He thought he was having a panic attack, but that thought only pinned him more firmly to the mattress. His chest went tight. His hands began to tremble. He felt like he was about to die. They'd find his body there, on that bed, in that sleazy hotel. He turned to face the woman and, with great effort, finally managed to speak. He begged her to distract him, to tell him a story to take his mind off that little girl's face, those eyes looking squarely into his own, those snuffed out black eyes, the eyes of his daughter, his beautiful daughter, buried in that dead girl's face.

The woman seemed lost for words, but after a while she began telling him how she was in her final year of university. She needed to pay off the student debt she'd racked up over her five-year degree. He listened and asked her to tell him something she'd learned that day. It's what he made his darling little girl do each night, his Julia, who that night, in that moment, was alive and sleeping soundly in her bed.

The woman didn't reply.

Please, he begged her.

She stood up, rearranged her skirt and picked up her jacket and purse.

The defining feature of a tragedy, she said then, is that we already know how it will end. We know from the outset that Oedipus has killed his father, slept with his mother and that eventually he'll go blind. And yet, for some reason, we carry on reading. Just like we carry on with our lives as if we don't already know the ending.

I could feel my throat cracking. The señor had his head in his hands to stop it rolling off onto the floor.

He asked me to bring him some more whisky, the bottle was almost empty. I took an unopened one from the larder, held it out to his glass and watched the golden liquid pour out. No glass had ever taken so long to fill. Time had never dragged as it did that morning.

And how *does* it end?

That's what the señor asked the woman from the hotel.

You lot already know the answer of course. Yes, you on the other side of the glass, sitting quietly in there as if it were possible not to squirm at a story like this. Don't make out like you can't see me. Don't pretend not to know. You know the ending, but he didn't, not yet.

I take your money and walk out of here, she said.

The señor nodded.

After that you lie there on the bed and you dissolve into laughter. You laugh so hard all the air floods back in to your lungs.

The señor nodded again.

Once you've pulled yourself together, you get up, go to the bathroom, splash your face, look up at the mirror and punch the glass, breaking it. Then you tear off the medicine cabinet door and with the sharpest piece of wood you can find you smash the sink in two. The destruction calms you down. Your strength calms you down. For a moment you feel good. Powerful. You don't notice the cut on your wrist until you get home, take a seat at the kitchen table and pour your heart out to your housemaid. Then you get drunk in front of her, you drink as much as your body can handle and you go to bed without dressing the wound that's already started to stain the white fabric of your good doctor's shirt.

The señor stood up and staggered from the kitchen into the hallway. Outside, the day had dawned. The red stain ran from his fist to his elbow. I'd never get it out, not even if I soaked it all day.

And then? he asked that woman again.

First you throw up, you make yourself sick. Then you lie down beside your wife but you don't touch her, no. You won't ever touch her again.

That can't be the ending, he said to the woman as she walked across the room. You said it was a tragedy.

Ask the question, she replied, removing all his bankcards, all his cash, and all his documents from his wallet.

Ask the question, she repeated, and without waiting to hear that question, she closed the door behind her.

I don't know what the question was. He didn't come out with it in the kitchen either. I don't think it matters when we already know the answer. The señor was staring at me. He could barely stand up. The whisky was pumping through his veins and his eyes were drowning in his own tears.

Do you know what the tragedy is, Estela? he said finally.

From somewhere down the hallway an alarm clock went off. It was seven in the morning.

Here's where the tragedy begins.

The señor didn't get out of bed that day. He told his wife he had a fever, a nasty cough, was tired from the night shift, and he holed himself up in his bedroom watching the news. At lunchtime he called for me and asked me to make him some broth. I tried my hardest not to look at him, and kept my eyes glued to the TV screen. A street vendor was shouting from the backseat of a police car on the news. I'm eighty years old, she was saying. I can't live off nothing. I have to work. Don't you throw away my goods. When I took the broth to the señor he reached out and held the tray firmly with two hands. He looked at me suspiciously, or so it seemed to me; he was worried about his secret. I let go of the tray, returned to the kitchen and the hours simply passed: washing the dishes, drying the dishes, putting away the dishes, starting again.

That night I went to bed especially tired, but I couldn't sleep. I was worried the señor would take another day off work and bump into Yany in the laundry room. And on top of that, his words, the tragedy, his secret were all haunting me. But then I said to myself: Estela, what else could possibly happen? Not knowing that the answer was: so much, and so quickly. I had no idea that life could do that: be put on pause for years and years and then make up for it in a matter of days.

I was just dozing off when I heard a scream followed by a rasping voice. It took me a while to recognise who it belonged to. The voice was trembling, but finally I placed it. The señor was saying:

Take everything. Everything.

I couldn't believe it. I lay there totally still. It was late at night and the objects around me were shrouded in the darkness. I was in darkness too, me and my voice, which is what saved us. The señor kept repeating, terrified:

Everything. Take everything.

From further away, the sound of the girl's occasional whimpers, the señora's absolute silence and the two men, because there were two of them, out of their minds screaming and shouting.

Hand over the money, fucker.

Where'd you keep the cash, you fucking fag?

Your phones, rich prick.

There was no money in that house. Not beyond whatever they, the señor and señora, happened to have in their wallet and purse.

Hand over your jewellery, bitch.

Your cards.

The diamonds.

Stop crying, you dumb bitch.

I said stop it, you little cry-baby.

I'll fucking rape you if you don't shut up.

I waited for them to leave, for the voices to disappear, but that didn't happen. I heard them enter the kitchen, rummage around in the drawers, open the cupboards. I could hear my own breath moving in and out. One heartbeat, another. And then the door to the back room slid open and the light from the kitchen, every last ray, flooded in and hit my face.

I didn't move. Covered in my blanket up to my neck, I pretended to be asleep, dead. Then I felt a hand grab my hair and yank it hard. I stood up from the bed, confused. I wasn't frightened, not as such; my heart was still beating at a normal pace, but I did feel scared when I saw the mask that was now in front of me. A black mask with no nose or mouth, just two holes for those jaded eyes.

The man was shaking uncontrollably, his teeth were chattering underneath the balaclava and he was blinking rapidly, as if trying to wake himself from that nightmare. He pulled my hair from side to side, out of his mind. I heard whole clumps being ripped from my scalp. Then he came right up in my face, as if he didn't believe what he was seeing. And I saw the sadness in those eyes and heard him say, in a whisper:

Give me the thirst.

At least that's what I think he said.

He was alone in there, alone with me, while the other man was busy smashing all the plates, all the glasses, all the serving dishes, which I would have to vigilantly sweep up so that the señor and señora didn't tread on any shards; so that the girl's delicate little feet didn't get cut to bloody shreds. I gazed at those eyes, which were the sole feature of his face. He spoke again.

Give me the thirst, he repeated.

I don't know why just then I had a flashback to my journey to Santiago all those years earlier: the stuffy, recycled air inside the bus and the young guy who got on in Temuco and didn't close his eyes the whole night. Big, black eyes, also sad and jaded. My mama had warned me not to leave the island. She'd told me to stay on the land, that even being poor down south was preferable to the alternative. It would be difficult, almost impossible, to quit working as a maid. It's a trap, she told me. You hang around waiting for a lucky break, and you secretly tell yourself: I'm leaving this week, next week for certain, next month will be my last here. And you just can't, Lita, that's what my mama warned me. You just can't leave. You can't ever say: Enough. You can't say: No, I've had it, Señora, my back hurts, I'm leaving. It's not like working in a shop or out in the fields doing the potato harvest. It's a job that's kept out of sight, that's what my mama said. And to top it off they accuse you of stealing, of eating too much, of washing your clothes in the same load as theirs. And in spite of everything, Lita, the inevitable happens. You grow fond of them, you know? That's people for you, my girl, that's what we're like. So don't go, listen to me. And if you do go, don't get attached. It's no good loving your masters. They only love their own.

I promised her I'd be back in a few months with a load of money. I promised her I'd buy her a flatscreen TV, some brand new trainers, a couple of cows, a few lambs. I'd extend the house, add another bathroom, a greenhouse. She shook her head as I prattled on. She called me stubborn, defiant, and she refused to wave me off at the station. She told me not to come back. Not to even visit.

The young guy on the bus was also going to Santiago. He'd landed a job as a security guard at a shopping centre. He would never work in the sawmills again. He felt bad for the pine trees and the great oaks that he himself felled with his chainsaw. He told me that in a couple of years he'd return to Temuco, rolling in it, and go and live on the mountain. He told me about a river there that only flowed in spring, and the horse he'd have, called Fifty.

I gazed out of the window and counted the roadside shrines illuminating the motorway. Soon the sun started to rise and my lips became parched from the dry northern air. He offered me a sip of his drink and half his mortadella roll. I took it, even though I wasn't hungry, and said: Fifty-fifty. He smiled, but the look in his eyes remained serious. When we reached Santiago he hurried off the bus and disappeared into the throng, and I realised that I hadn't even asked him his name. There are two types of people in this world: those who have a name, and those who don't. And only those without names can disappear.

I felt a stabbing pain in my neck from where the intruder was still yanking my hair. I tried to stand up straight, push him away, make him stop. It didn't work. Through his balaclava I could see the outline of his cheekbones, the marked curve of his jaw and the relief of his eyebrows. I desperately wanted to know what was underneath that mask. Who that kid was. What he wanted from me.

Without thinking I reached out my hand and touched the fabric, and, beneath it, those jutting bones. He was taken aback, suddenly passive, as if no one had ever touched him. Then, starting from his neck, I slowly began to lift his balaclava. It felt like I was ripping a scab from his scalp.

I peeled off the mask and dropped it at our feet. Almost a child, he was. A child and yet not really a child. A being who had not for one second known childhood.

We stayed like that for some time. My hand touching his warm face, my fingers on his chin. Outside, the sound of smashing glass made me jump. The boy seemed to wake up suddenly, and he grabbed my wrist tightly, moved right into my face and said in my ear:

Open your mouth.

My legs and arms went stiff and my fingers cramped. I clenched my teeth and pressed my lips together. What did that man want? Who was he?

Open your fucking mouth.

I felt cold. A kind of cold that merited a different name. The boy was whispering. He never once shouted at me. He spoke in a hushed voice, just for me and him, as if we were sharing a secret. He was about my height, he came up to here, right here, but he was much thinner than me. And that slight body, brimming with hatred, brimming with sadness, was also trembling. His whole being was quaking.

Open it. Fucking open it.

On the other side of the door, in the kitchen, I could hear the girl's muffled sobs and from the señora and the señor: silence. A silence totally different to my own. They were dumbstruck, the pair of them, perhaps marginally calmer now that the target was the maid in her nightshirt, the maid standing stiff as a board, her eyes open, her mouth clamped shut.

Fucking bitch.

That's what the man-child called me.

And then:

Open your fucking mouth or I'll put a hole in your snout.

I thought he was going to kill me. I thought I was about to die. And it was so strange, that thought. The idea that the man-child would put a bullet in my head actually calmed me down. I pictured my mama, her leathery hands, her spotless skin at bedtime, and I thought about how in my memory she was safe from harm, she would always be safe from harm, and how I would soon be with her in the faraway place where she was waiting for me.

So I parted my lips. I opened my mouth. And I looked him in the eyes, ready to feel the cold touch of the gun and then nothing, nothing, nothing ever again.

I looked at him serenely. And he looked at me. Our eyes met and I could feel the tears running down the sides of my face. He leaned back, hawked up a mouthful of phlegm and spat in my mouth.

Fucking slave.

That's what he said.

Then he ran out of the room, grabbed the other guy by the arm and together they left the house.

The police arrived a few hours later. The girl was sleeping in her parents' bed, curled up like she was a baby, while everyone else stood talking around the dining-room table.

They took a statement from the señor. He didn't mention that the previous night his bankcards had been stolen, or that his wallet had contained documents showing his address. He didn't tell them, either, that he knew who might be behind the attack. He didn't say much, but the señora spoke for both of them.

As she finished giving her statement, I worried they'd make me do the same. Make me tell them about the man-child's gappy teeth or how the corners of his mouth curled upwards, as if he were still capable of happiness. None of this happened. When what should have been my turn came around and I stood wondering if I was capable of speaking, if I'd be able to find the words, instead they read out the señora's statement. The eldest officer asked me if it was accurate, and, without waiting for my answer, held out the piece of paper it was written on for me to sign:

'Estela García, forty years old, single, domestic worker. Claims no physical harm committed against her during the assault. Signs the above made statement.'

After that, for some reason he put a tiny piece of cotton wool in my mouth and took a sample of saliva.

The gun arrived a week or so later. Days in which the señor became obsessed with martial arts lessons, self-defence techniques, ways to kill a person with his bare hands. Obsessed with getting stronger, with fighting, with defending what was rightfully his. Luckily it didn't occur to him to buy a German Shepherd, which would have pushed Yany out for good. Instead he opted for the simpler solution of a handgun with which to shoot any thieving bastards in the eye. He'd make sure no one could ever frighten the doctor, the man of the house, like that again: to the point of wetting himself in front of his daughter, in front of his wife, in front of the maid.

I was spring cleaning. Shaking out the rugs. Washing the curtains. Replacing last season's clothes with this season's. Moving it all from one wardrobe to another. From one drawer to another. Yany was asleep in the laundry room having drunk her water and eaten her bread. She'd gone sniffing around the kitchen when she'd arrived – every last corner, every last piece of furniture, as if those men were still there. The girl was at school and the señor and señora at their respective jobs. My mama was still dead. On the TV in the master bedroom some fishermen were declaring a strike. There were no more tollos or sea bass to catch. They were demanding the trawlers leave their fishing zones. They don't leave us anything, one of them was saying, they even kill the whales. I spotted a whale once, its black fin poking out of the water. At first I thought it was a piece of old tyre, but my mama told me to wait. Nothing is ever what it seems, Lita. That's what she said. Then, suddenly, the whale leapt out of the water.

I was finishing clearing out the wardrobe, lost in my memories again, when I noticed what I thought was a lone sock at the very back of a drawer. But the fabric was slippery. I pulled whatever it was towards me, removed the handkerchief wrapped around it and found myself with a gun in my right hand. Have you ever held a gun? They're heavy enough to bend back your wrist, your arm. The whole room bent to offset the weight of that thing.

As an image I found it confusing. It's hard to explain. My hand, with its cracked and gnarled knuckles, was holding a solid and indisputably real handgun. I placed my finger on the trigger, held out my arm and aimed at the closet. There was the señor's blue coat, his elegant black suits, his white, grey, pink and pale blue shirts, his good doctor's white coat, and there was that dress, the black one, the one that the señora never ended up wearing because it made her look cheap. Or because her maid had tried it on. I ran the gun through those hanging clothes and could almost feel their textures on my fingertips. Then, without thinking, I brought the muzzle to my temple.

The cold feel of the metal was unsettling, but what truly terrified me was the steam coming from the barrel of the gun, as if it had already been fired and my corpse left lying on the master bedroom floor. I didn't even question whether or not it was loaded; I just assumed it was. The gun had five bullets in it, and a mere jolt of my finger would be enough to send one of them through my skull. I pressed down lightly with my fingertip. I felt hot and cold. Hot and cold at the same time.

It's a curious thing that we are all going to die, don't you think? All of us, even you. There's no point wondering if we will, because the answer is always the same. Be it your mother, your father, your dog, your cat, your daughter, your son, the chincol, the thrush, your husband or your wife – the answer is always the same: yes, yes, yes. There are only two unanswered questions: how and when. And that gun answered them with absolute certainty.

The gun belonged to the señor, to the señor's fear. I had witnessed the terror in his eyes the night of the assault. Perhaps that was why he detested me. Because by now his maid had seen too much. I'd seen him fucking his wife, I'd seen him naked in the bedroom, I'd seen him fear for his very life. And he was more frightened than his wife. More frightened than his daughter. And considerably more frightened than his domestic servant.

I wrapped the gun back up in the handkerchief, but as I went to put it back in its hiding place, I changed my mind. And I took it, that's right. I took the gun to the back room and I hid it under the mattress. In case one day, one afternoon, I got the urge to answer those two questions: how and when.

The alarm people showed up that same week. The girl had started wetting the bed, so to help her feel safe and like the house was hers again they contacted a security company. The señora said:

Estela, open the door to them.

And then:

Keep an eye on them, do you hear? Don't let them out of your sight.

There was no need for me to answer. Maybe there never would be again. My mama had warned me: It's a trap, Lita. But my mama was dead. My mama was still dead. And that's a trap no one escapes from.

They got out of a van carrying two toolboxes and a length of barbed wire which they unrolled around the entire boundary railing. I didn't see when or how they connected it to the electricity. The señora and the girl were at the supermarket and the señor in a meeting. I went and sat at the kitchen table to chop cabbage and grate carrots.

With the external wire installed, they knocked on the front door. Inside, they mounted sensors on the living-room ceiling, motion spotlights in the garden, and a camera pointing to the front of the property. They told me to sign at the bottom of a piece of paper and I did. One of them was very tall with a slightly hunched back, and as I wrote my name, he said:

Anyone tries to get over that wall they'll be fried like an egg.

He flashed a set of tartar-covered teeth and I noticed that the sides of his mouth were turned down.

That night, the señora tried out the new security system. She said that the alarm code would be 2-2-2-2. She showed me how to set and unset it, and then she asked me to prepare a couple of steaks.

Nice and thick, she said, so they stay juicy.

I plunged the tip of the knife into the plastic wrapping around the meat and the metallic stench of blood wafted through the kitchen. Then a fly landed on my hand. I'm not going off on another tangent. The fly is important.

I ignored it as best I could and placed the beef tenderloin on the chopping board. The blade sliced through the fat and sinew until it met with the solid wood. My mind wandered to the slash marks on the board and I wondered if it would ever be possible not to notice those scars. Tomatoes. Chicken. Peppers. Onion. One slash on top of another, on top of another, on top of another. Messages from the women who came before me. Warnings for those who'd follow.

I left the two raw steaks on a plate and was going to season them when I realised that the salt had run out. There was none in the shaker, none in the little bowl where some was usually kept, and none in the larder. A whole kilo of salt, all used up. Do you see what I'm getting at? Do you know how much time is contained in a kilo of salt? Weeks and weeks of my mama being dead and me sprinkling salt on their salads, salt on their scrambled eggs, salt on their buttered salmon. We'd gone through another kilo of salt and I was still in that house.

I swallowed hard, feeling sick. The fly was resting on an offcut of fat. Its head was iridescent and it was rubbing its black, kinked legs. I waved my hand to shoo it away, but it flew right back to its perch. I flapped my hand again, it took off noisily and just when I thought it had gone, it flew like a shot into my eyes. I closed them and flapped my hands about but now the fly was trying to get into my ear. Into both ears. I could feel its wings against my eyelids, its paws rubbing against my eardrums. In a frenzy, I backed away. One step, two.

I don't know what I tripped on but the next thing I knew I felt a blow to the back of my head and something warm in the palm of my hand. When I opened my eyes I was on the kitchen floor. The fly was settled on my knee, rubbing its legs obsessively, and my hand was gripping the warm, red knife blade.

I tried to stand up but I couldn't. I felt dizzy, with a horrible taste at the back of my throat. The white ceiling above bore down on me, my head was throbbing. I had blood on my hand, a gash on my palm, a fly on my knee, a gob of spit in my mouth, a mother buried somewhere. Everything around me was spinning. Then I heard this noise:

Tick.

Tick.

Tick.

I'm not sure you'll have ever noticed it before. Probably not. Maybe my silence also made it seem louder.

I took several deep breaths to help me calm down. I got up slowly, rinsed my hand, cleaned the wound and washed the blood from the knife blade. Afterwards, I cooked the beef steaks and dressed the salad, without a pinch of salt. I didn't reply when they said that the food was under-seasoned. I could only think about that sound:

Tick.

Tick.

Tick.

Like a time bomb.

The girl, during those final days, was especially restless. The señora didn't want her to go to school in the week following the break-in. She thought it was wise to wait, but the señor talked her around. It was important to get back to routine. To avoid falling behind. To act normally. Get on with it. He took her to school himself the first day, but two hours later the girl was back with stomach cramps and a rash.

I let her sit in the kitchen in front of the TV, even though the señora had forbidden her from watching any before doing her homework. There was a programme about animals on. Some elephants who, every year, migrated to a grotto, always the same one, where they would lick the minerals on the cave walls and then drop dead. Yany, meanwhile, was dozing in the laundry room doorway. The girl seemed to cheer up on seeing her, and instinctively she went over to stroke her, but she must have remembered the faint scars on her calf because she didn't get any closer. I know it was a mistake to let the girl see her, but I didn't have the heart to throw the dog out. Meanwhile, the eldest elephant in the herd was pulling away from the others, wandering down a bamboo trail and eventually lying down under a black sky to await its death.

The girl looked away from the screen and asked me why I wasn't afraid.

I didn't reply.

The other elephants carried on their way without turning back. They were walking a little slower now, a little mournfully or hesitantly maybe, but still unquestionably onward.

I saw you, she said. You pulled down his mask, Nana.

I went over to the girl, crouched down beside her and stroked her head. Her plait had come loose, like a textile unravelling.

What did his face look like?

I wanted to remember that face but I couldn't. I could only see my mama's: those rosy lips, her eyes full of gentleness, her rounded, wonky teeth.

The girl asked again why I hadn't been afraid.

My daddy wet himself, she said. He did a wee-wee in his trousers, I saw it.

I gently undid her French plait and began a new one, from the crown of her head, lock by lock. Once I'd finished, I kissed her forehead and asked myself if I'd miss her. If once I'd left I'd miss those impertinent questions of hers.

Why do you not talk, Nana?

Of course I'd miss her. In the way you miss a habit until another one replaces it.

I made her a banana milkshake and a piece of toast and jam, but she didn't touch either. She said she wasn't hungry, that she didn't ever want to eat again. She looked emaciated, puffy-eyed, and her gaze was impenetrable, hopeless. I tried to remember the moment her face had changed. She looked tired and defeated. As if she'd lived for long enough.

The banana milkshake turned brown and when the señora got in from work she poured it down the drain. The woman stood there for a moment, looking at the stringy fibres of the fruit stuck in the plug hole, as if the drain contained the answer to her daughter's problems, the way out of that dead-end street.

A while later, with one eye on the television, the señora prepared herself a salad with seeds. Lamb's lettuce and seeds. Chicory and seeds. A special news bulletin was just starting. Roads shut off. Barricades. Hundreds of hooded faces. Lootings. Fires.

I looked up. There were protests in Santiago, Antofagasta, Valparaíso, Osorno, Puerto Montt, Punta Arenas. The screen was divided into six frames, all identical apart from one in which a journalist was interviewing a bleary eyed woman:

They want us to roll over on our backs, she said, staring into the camera.

The señora stood gawping at the news as she ate. Once she'd calmly finished her salad, she cleared her throat, frowned and shook her head. On the screen a group of people were dragging car tyres across a street to block it off.

The señor came over to see what was happening. The pair of them were concerned. There had been protests down at the lumberyard too. Even some of the admin staff at the clinic had joined the marches. Discontent, they said. I could hear the scene: she and him arguing in front of the TV. My two bosses, the fires raging on the screen, the hooded faces. Having no faces at all, those bodies seemed to share the same face. That's what I thought, or I might not have got to the end of that thought because just then the señora switched off the TV, somewhat irked, somewhat irritated, although I knew beneath all that lay fear.

As soon as they left the kitchen that sound outside came back – tick, tick, tick – but I ignored it. The girl had another meltdown, screaming and shouting in the hallway, although she soon exhausted herself. The señora contemplated that exhausted, washed-out little girl, sapped of energy, always on the verge of tears, and she went over to say something to her husband.

It's not normal, she said.

He waved her away. He was on the phone.

It was only one or two afternoons later. Although who can really say.

I was in the laundry room, separating the whites from the colours: the white towels, the white pants, the white vests. It was Monday, make a note of that. I know it was because every Monday all of the sheets in the house were changed. There I go again with 'were changed'. On Mondays *I* changed all of the sheets, pulled them off the beds, threw them in the washing machine and watched them sink under the water's weight. A crushing weight, have you ever thought about it? A potentially lethal weight. Even for someone strong and proficient. Someone who knows how to swim. I don't know how to swim, have you made a note of that too? And yet I dived right in when I saw Julia floating on the water.

Yany was snoring, curled up on one side of the laundry room. Serene. Trusting. In a place far from reality. The girl was watching TV at full volume in the kitchen. Her parents were at work. It was a peaceful, normal day.

I was finishing hanging out the sheets when the girl came to the laundry room and asked me why they had to celebrate her birthday. It was coming up soon and her mother had promised to throw her a fancy-dress party. She'd already bought her dress. The other children would all dress up as superheroes, monsters and animals, and she wouldn't be able to recognise them underneath their masks. She wanted to know how we knew that the bad men wouldn't come. Then she fell quiet, as if pondering something important, and she asked me why that man, the one with the mask, hated her dad so much, why he hated her mum.

Does he hate me too, Nana?

That's what she wanted to know.

I was still pulling the sheets taut to prevent them from drying with creases. If they dried on the line with any sort of fold then not even the iron would press it out. It was important to hang the fabric as taut as possible. The girl became upset when I didn't answer. She started shouting, screaming and kicking me in the legs. She was hungry and tired and in a panic, that girl. She wanted to know why we had to throw a party when she didn't even want to get older; why she would have to wear that white princess dress.

She was beside herself, her face all screwed up. And I asked myself at that moment exactly when the girl had fallen into such a total state of despair.

Why the masks, Nana?

Why? Why?

Why won't you talk to me? she said.

Say something, she ordered.

Say something or I'll tell on you, Nana.

That was a caution. I looked into her eyes and believed I could see straight through her: to her fear, her anxiety, her boundless arrogance. I could have replied: You little shit, you spoiled brat, you rude little girl. Something to put her in her place. By that point, though, my voice was already too far away.

Yany's ears pricked up at the sound of the child's threats and she sat on her hind legs, suddenly alert.

I'm going to tell on you, the girl said, running inside the house.

Yany flopped back down, rested her head on the floor and closed her eyes. She looked older, and I thought: Older like you, Estela. You've aged too. And then I knew with absolute clarity that I had to get out of that place as soon as possible. My mama no longer needed the money. I could take the dog with me; that docile mutt who liked to doze near the drying bedsheets with their shade sweeping over her dull old coat.

I suppose I must have been so lost in that thought that I didn't hear her come in. I didn't hear the car, or her keys, or her high heels making their way across the kitchen. Only a shriek and then my name, spoken in a voice covered in thorns.

Estela.

That's what the señora said when she came across that unfamiliar dog, that insolent, ordinary, potentially dangerous bitch who then jumped up on all fours and bared her worn old teeth.

What on earth is all this? What were you thinking? the señora said, incandescent with rage, and I noticed the hairs on Yany's back were standing on end and her eyes were full of fear.

The girl was standing next to her mother with a sneering look on her face. An expression somewhere between angry and vengeful, which for a moment made her look like an adult. She and her mother glared at me with identical expressions and I saw that the corners of their mouths, both of them, had started to turn downwards.

Yany retreated and pressed her body right up against the laundry room wall. I remember she looked at me with a wounded expression, as if I had broken a promise. The señora, meanwhile, was trying to back her into a corner with her body. She kept clapping, opening her arms and shouting:

Out, dog! Out!

She was steering Yany towards the exit, away from her property, away from her daughter.

The dog retraced her steps with her ribs pressed against the wall and padding down the connecting passageway between the laundry room and the front garden. The señora, the girl and I all followed her.

Out in the front garden, a few metres from the gate, Yany stopped. I didn't know what to do, how to explain to Yany that this wasn't my house, it wasn't my decision. She had frozen, the dog, just before the gate, too scared to move and escape.

The señora lost her patience and bellowed:

Estela, take care of it!

And then:

Get out of here, dog! Out! out!

Yany stood bewildered and stock-still. The girl, in response to all the yelling, started to sob. The señora was flapping her arms wildly when, suddenly, she also froze. She looked at the hose, then at the dog. She'd made her decision.

Aiming the hose at Yany's chest, she turned the tap on fully open. Soaked, my Yany was soaked, and immediately she started to bark. It was a sad, desperate baying that broke my heart, but didn't stop the señora. She aimed the spraying water directly at Yany's eyes and the dog, her eyelids half-open, sopping wet, unsure what to do, finally gave up and slipped through the bars of the gate.

Time stopped. Write that down in your reports. Time came to a halt, or maybe I got left outside of it and time just carried on without me. Because just as Yany was about to leave the property, still half-in and half-out with her tail inside the garden and her head out on the pavement, we all heard – the señora, the girl and I – that sound: no longer a tick but a crack, like a whip. It came from the electric fence, from the high voltage cables, from the barbed wire crowning the boundary walls. And with that sound flew red, yellow and white sparks.

The lights flickered along the entire block and then cut out. I was amazed by the silence that followed. Gone was the noise, that ticking sound I'd been hearing for days. A few seconds later the lights came back on. The alarms of the nearby houses all went off at once. All the other dogs began to howl in response to the terrible, high-pitched sound.

I put my hand up to my mouth, as if a word were trying to come out and I was holding it back. I fell to my knees beside Yany, who was now unconscious on the ground with her head on the pavement and the rest of her body still inside the front garden. I touched her then, on the belly, and could feel her breathing. She was still warm, alive. She'd survived.

The girl started sobbing hysterically. The señora shouted:

Don't touch her, Estela! You could be electrocuted.

Her voice sounded muffled, as if it were coming from deep underwater. I leaned forward, reached between the bars and with my two hands I picked up Yany's head to look at her face. She had gone. Yany no longer inhabited those eyes and in her place was a plea, a desperate appeal for help. She was dying. Her breathing had become heavy. My dog was about to die. The girl wouldn't stop crying. The señora was shouting at her to go inside, she absolutely shouldn't witness that. But the girl, that girl, had to see.

I kissed Yany's big head and hoped she'd die right there and then. Enough, I thought, enough, that's enough now, but that thought alone couldn't put an end to her suffering.

It was as if my body were moving on its own, my body without me, because at no point did I leave Yany's side. I never stopped stroking her, never abandoned her, but that woman, the one I had been in the past, stood up, strode to the back room and felt around for the handgun under the mattress.

I returned to the fence holding that gun, which no longer seemed so heavy or solid, but perfect. And yes, of course I thought about killing her, putting a bullet in the señora's heart and letting her die there in her garden, with her gun, murdered by her maid in full view of her only child.

I stood beside Yany and could see her belly shuddering. I looked at her for the last time, blinked very slowly and, without a second thought, aimed between her ears, unlocked the gun and put a bullet in the smooth little head of that docile dog. Now and forevermore a good dog.

Her blood was splattered on my uniform and the sudden loud noise startled a flock of thrushes. A shudder ran through me, too. As if, all at once, I'd woken up.

Now, my friends, I'd like your full attention. I think at this point I've said enough to be able to call you what I like. If you are over there then stop whatever you're doing. I know I've taken my time; I know that sometimes it must have seemed like I was taking you all around the houses, but what can you do. How can you recognise the main road without the odd detour?

Sometimes the facts present themselves a little hazily. That's all because of words, you know? Words detach themselves from the facts and then it's impossible to name them. That's what happened to me in that house; the silence brought everything crashing down. The simplest of thoughts fell apart; routine actions, like how to swallow without choking, how to expel the air from my lungs, how to muster the next heartbeat, melted away. When that happens, it becomes very hard to make sense of reality. When there are no words, do you follow? Without words there can be no order, no past or present. We have no way, for example, of asking objects or animals if they can see us, whether the willows and the cacti and the cardinals can see us, or if it really is just we who see them and foist names onto them: willow, cactus, cardinal. We don't know if they stop existing when we stop speaking of them, or if the world goes on intact and silent.

I know you won't understand me. I know it's difficult, baffling even, but just think about the sun. I can never get my head around it, its purpose, its motive, why it's so persistent, why it pushes on, as it does, the sun, every day, every morning, the sun, the sun, the sun. Just thinking about the sun makes my head spin: even on a cloudy day, even at night-time when it disappears, the sun goes on being true. An insane truth. A truth beyond what is visible to me, beyond words. And you, my friends ... how am I to understand you? Are you like the sun, or do you disappear when I stop talking? And what do you make of yourselves when you're not here, when you're shaving in front of the mirror or buttoning up your shirts? Or when you put on your makeup and apply your lipstick to appear slightly different? Who are you? How do you dress? What are your voices like? What kind of person is capable of hiding behind a wall and passing judgement on another without showing their own face?

The events happened without warning, let me be perfectly clear. And without warning it's very difficult, almost impossible, to avert them.

The girl tried to stifle her sobs but couldn't.

Is she dead? she asked, her face wet with tears.

The señora nodded and said:

Yes.

The girl looked at the gun, at my hand, at the blood, at the dog. It was then, in that moment, that the idea was born. I have absolutely no doubt about it. A dark idea that wormed its way deep inside the fertile mind of that child.

The señora snatched the gun from my hand and somehow managed to unload it. Four bullets fell onto the freshly cut lawn. The fifth was now inside the limp, motionless body of my Yany. The señora took the girl in her arms and headed towards the house, but just before entering, she turned around and said:

The animal, take care of it.

And then:

I'll call someone to come and take it away.

I looked at her for what felt like a very long second. Yany wasn't moving. She wasn't breathing. She wasn't barking. She wasn't grunting. Alive-dead. That's what I thought. And in the line connecting those two words, barely the blink of an eye. My Yany alive-my Yany dead. My mama alive-my mama dead. Death, I thought, meant becoming pure past. It meant never again falling ill. It was simple, quick. Death wasn't horrible, do you understand? It never had been. What was horrible, truly horrifying, was the act of dying.

I went to get a bin bag from the larder then returned to the front garden, knelt down beside Yany and put her inside it. She seemed incredibly heavy, which is why I ended up dragging her to the laundry room. Once there, I left her on the floor to one side of the ironing board. The next morning someone would come for her. A man wearing gloves who would pick up her body and drive her away in a van. I pictured her burning body, the smell, the flames. I felt sick then. I feel sick again now.

I don't know why I hung back waiting for the police to arrive. Maybe I thought a neighbour would have called them after hearing the gunshot, but the police don't come out for a dead dog. Eventually I left the kitchen and returned to the back room. And as I washed my hands in the bathroom, as I scrubbed my nails, my cuticles, each and every finger, each and every crack until they were clean, spotless, the señora poked her head into the room for the last time. And from the threshold of that glass door, of her glass door, in her house, in her neighbourhood, in her country, on her planet, she talked and she talked and she talked.

You're insane, that's what she said.

I didn't reply.

You've lost your mind, Estela. What were you thinking?

I don't recall what else she said, but I do remember that behind her the television was showing the protests in the centre of town, the blockades in Valparaíso and the mass marches on the bridge in Ancud. There, in the distance, was the channel connecting the mainland to the island. And further inland, in the middle of the open countryside, my mama's house. I was supposed to be there, not in Santiago.

The girl had told the señora everything. That the dog had been coming over for months. That she was called Yany. That weeks earlier she had bitten her on the calf. She told her about the fat pink rat, about the blood that had poured from her wounded leg. She told her that the nana had forced her to clean the kitchen floor. That she'd made her promise to keep the secret. That she'd cleaned the wound with a piece of cotton wool dipped in alcohol. The señora must have looked at those two scars in total disbelief. Then came the shouting, unbroken shouting, after which she calmed down. Finally, she told me that she would pay me an extra month but that I was to leave as soon as possible, she didn't ever want to see me again.

You'll go first thing tomorrow, that's what the señora Mara López said.

Once she'd run out of steam, a few hours later, it was the señor's turn.

He walked into the kitchen and, without even looking at me, from the other side of the sliding glass door, he told me that he'd left my cheque on the worktop.

There's a limit, he said.

There was a limit for everything.

The cheque didn't move from there, go ahead and ask. You, I'm talking to you. A cheque for one month so that in precisely thirty days' time I would go and find myself another job, go and scrub the crusty shit off another toilet bowl, in another house, for another good family.

I woke up at three in the morning. Or it's possible I was already awake and that was just another sleepless night of many. I sat up on the bed and had the following thought: It's been seven years, seven Christmases, seven New Years since you came. You were seven years younger, your hands softer, your voice too.

Switching on the bedside lamp I looked for these very clothes: this black skirt, this white blouse and these plim-solls with the worn-down soles. I let down my hair and brushed it out. The tips lightly touched my waist and that contact felt strange to me. As if I were a stranger inside that room: that other woman, seven years younger, the one who had looked in those drawers on her first day of work and discovered the uniforms with their fake top buttons: Monday, Tuesday, Wednesday, Thursday, Friday, Saturday.

I walked across the front garden and into the street. The branches of the sweetgum trees were brushing against the streetlight, forming flickering shadows down on the ground. It seemed strange to have lived for so long in that house and never to have noticed those shadows, their shapes on the tarmac. In the south I knew with my eyes closed the call of every insect, the footsteps of the vultures on the roof and the trees' shadows at night when the moon was full. It was the first time I'd walked down that street at that hour. The first and last, I thought.

I hadn't foreseen coming across Carlos. I didn't go out looking for him. I just needed to clear my head, get some air, think. Or maybe die, you know? Maybe I wanted a car to lose control and smash into my legs. A head-on, fatal collision that would let me seal the trio of deaths: my mama, Yany and me. The perfect ending to this story. But I didn't come across a single car on the road and, instead, there was Carlos. He was sitting in front of the petrol station, rocking on his seat. The night was clear and clean as if nothing bad had taken place, as if nothing more could happen. I watched as the burning red tip of his cigarette lit up the edges of his mouth. The image stuck in my mind: man with mouth, man without mouth. And, for some reason, I was determined to go and speak to him.

He didn't see me when I came off the pavement, or when I walked across the petrol station forecourt, dodging the rubber hoses and the empty bins. He didn't even see me when I was one step away from his seat, and for a second I doubted I was actually there. Maybe a car had run me over, or maybe I was still in the back room, trying to sleep, and it was all just a nightmare. One from which I'd never wake.

I've always liked the smell of petrol; I don't know if I've mentioned this already. How it climbs behind your forehead and spreads out, filling everything. I smelled that smell then immediately felt a terrible thirst. A thirst like the one I've had ever since you locked me up in this place. No one should ever have to feel a thirst like this. Not you, and not me either. A thirst that made me want to put the nozzle of one of those hoses in my mouth, press the trigger and let the petrol rush down my throat.

I was one step away from Carlos, almost directly in front of him, when he caught me. I caught a flicker of fear in his eyes and was relieved that he could see me.

What's wrong? he asked, jumping up out of his seat.

He was barely taller than me. From further away, on my trips to the supermarket, he'd always seemed quite stocky, but in reality he was skinny and slight, an overgrown kid in those overalls and with that grease stain in the middle of his chest. What kind of person rubs dirt over their heart? What kind of man, I thought, looking him up and down.

Once he'd got over his surprise, he smiled at me and started talking again.

Are you okay? he asked, his voice full of tenderness.

Did they do something to you? Is Daisy okay?

I couldn't remember the last time I'd heard my own voice, or someone had asked me how I was. On the other end of the telephone, my mama would always, without fail, ask me that question. How are you, trouble? Why don't you come home, you stubborn old mule? I didn't know how to answer Carlos. I didn't know if they'd done something to me. When? What?

The streetlamps were giving off a faint, dirty glow. It was a hot night. Carlos's face was gleaming. I noticed his serious, sightly weary expression. The look of someone who's worked more than their fair share. He had a few grey hairs, the first, on his right sideburn. Premature white hairs for a premature tiredness. I stepped closer and touched them, convinced that he wouldn't be able to feel me. I know this will sound strange, but it's what I thought: that my silence had made not only my voice disappear, but my skin too, and that he wouldn't be able to see or feel me.

Straight away I could feel he was sweating, and I was surprised to find the pads of my fingers were damp. I wondered if I would also start to sweat, if his body would heat mine. Carlos didn't wait for my answer. How was I supposed to know if I was okay, if Yany was okay.

He brought his face close to mine and I could feel his breath. Tobacco, hunger, a faint whiff of alcohol.

Estela, he said.

I liked hearing my name in his voice, hearing it come out of his mouth. He took another step to get even closer, held my chin in his hand and looked at me head on. My chest pressed against the stain on his overalls. He had large eyes, Carlos, brimming with hopeful anticipation. For some reason I wanted to close mine.

He leaned his body into mine and hitched up my skirt. I heard it rip on one side. Here, see? I didn't want to ruin this skirt, but Carlos ripped it just here. A tear that I'd have to mend. With a needle and thread, I'd have to patiently sew up this skirt.

He hiked it up, now completely torn, right to my waist. Then he did the same with my knickers but in the opposite direction, pulling them down to my ankles in one swift motion. I heard the zip of his overalls and could feel his chest pressing against my own. His body was firm, warm, and I liked the feel of it against me. Sweat was dripping from my forehead. I felt even thirstier, even hotter. Carlos nudged my legs apart with his legs and pushed inside of me. He rocked back and forth. I could hear both of our breathing and his grunting in my ear. Gentle, serene grunting, which somehow made me feel sad.

When he'd finished, I turned around and pulled up my knickers. It was still night. That interminable night. He wanted to hold me, for me to stay.

What's the rush? he said while I rearranged my clothes.

He didn't know anything. He would never know anything. There are people who go through life not knowing, with the corners of their mouths intact.

He zipped up the fly on his overalls and I watched the black stain reappear over his heart. A shadow, I thought. The shadow of his heart. And with that, I turned and headed back to the house.

I walked the whole way in the middle of the streets, and although no cars or animals came near me, when I reached the front gate, I couldn't move. It seemed unimaginable to me that the key in my hand would open that door. I couldn't believe that to one side of it, over in the bushes, was that gap and the evidence of Yany's death. I recalled my hands, these hands, bagging up her corpse. These very hands leaving her on her own in the laundry room. It had all been real. It's all still real.

You might not understand. Maybe you still have no idea what I'm talking about. Have you never stared so intensely at an object that the edges of reality start to vibrate? Have you never said a word so many times it starts to fall apart? Try it, go on. Let's see if you can finally get the difference between reality and unreality.

Yany. Yany. Yany. Yany. Yany. Yany. Yany. Yany.

Yany was dead. My mama was dead. But death always, without exception, comes in threes.

I don't know what time it must have been. Four, five. It was still the middle of the night. The señora was sleeping. Beside her, the señor was sleeping soundly. In her own bedroom, the girl. I, on the other hand, wouldn't go back to sleep. And there were others like me and Carlos who didn't sleep at night either.

I walked to the shed, looked for a shovel, then returned to the front garden. Directly in front of the gap where Yany used to come in and out, where I myself had killed her, I started to dig a hole. The ground was rocky and resistant. I kept going until I could feel my neck damp with sweat. I had barely scratched the surface and yet exhaustion forced me to stop. I looked down at the gravelly ground, at the shovel in my hand. This wasn't her place. This couldn't be her place.

I went out into the street, looked around and immediately spotted a patch of earth at the foot of the ceibo in full bloom. I started to dig a deep, suitably wide hole to one side of its roots. There, on the street, in what had always been her home. It took me a good while to dig that hole. Every thrust of the shovel hurt. Nobody seemed to hear me. Once I'd finished I went to the laundry room, picked up the bin bag and carried her outside. Then I removed her body from the bag and lay her gently at the bottom of the hole, as if it were still possible to hurt her.

I stood there for a long time looking at her brown coat, her jutting bones, her curved back, the little pads of her black, calloused paws. Then I covered her with earth, more and more, until my Yany disappeared.

Standing up, I shook off the dirt and noticed that the stars were fading. The sky was changing colour from black to an intense violet. I saw the mountain range emerge out of darkness and it occurred to me that, even though it was barely visible, even though I rarely looked at it, the mountain continued to be true. It would always be true, whoever looked at it. And perhaps, somewhere inside a deeper, truer darkness, my mama and Yany would also always be true.

I entered the house and put the kettle on to make a tea. The last tea before leaving. It was then, as I flicked on the switch, that I heard the noise. A strange sound, like water churning. At first I thought that the kettle had broken. The señora would have to buy a new one. I could almost hear her voice: Estela, not again, you are a butterfingers. But then I heard the noise a second time. It was coming from the back garden.

I went into the dining room, not really thinking anything. Doesn't that seem strange to you? I went in there not expecting to see anything, and it was only when I looked through the double doors that I spotted it: a white dot in the middle of the water.

Are you paying attention? If you are, then write this down; this is what you came to hear.

At first I didn't trust my eyes. I hadn't slept all night and the sun had just come up, which is probably why I thought: You're tired, you're sad, it's nothing, it can't be. The girl is asleep, I told myself, in her bed, in her pale blue pyjamas, with her plait coming loose. I think then I blinked several times, as if I couldn't believe what I was seeing. It looked like a mistake, do you know what I mean? A white form floating on the water, hair rippling like a sinister petrol stain. She was face down with her arms spread wide. And it was as if all that motionless water were gazing back at me.

A few seconds passed, or it might have been longer than that. Seconds like hours. Days like years. I was frozen to my spot on the other side of the window. And this much I can confess to: my reaction wasn't the quickest. I could only think one thing, a single invasive thought tapping away in my head. The girl would soon be waking up, at which point I'd have to brush her hair, coax her into eating some bread, get her shoes on. But if she went plunging to the bottom of the pool on me, if she drowned out there in the garden, I'd get behind and wouldn't have time to warm up her milk, plait her hair, prepare her parents' breakfast and put away the mugs with the mugs, the spoons with the spoons, the knives with the knives. It was that thought that upset me. And then, finally, I saw her. I saw the body of the girl lying face down in the swimming pool.

Instinctively, I raced outside and dived straight in. Dressed in these plimsolls, this skirt, this top, and with my long hair loose, I sank down into the water. That's right: the woman who had looked after that girl for seven years, who had changed her nappies, tied her laces and scrubbed her armpits, who had wiped her bottom, played with her – the cleaning woman, the nana, the one who couldn't swim – she dived headlong into the swimming pool.

The water was all around me, rushing into my mouth and up my nose. I thrashed about, flapped my arms and opened my eyes down there. Shadows, that's what I saw, and the girl's dark outline. I was drowning, do you understand? I was also on the brink of death. My kicking feet found nothing but water, only water between my toes. It was a curious moment. Curious that I didn't feel any fear. All I felt was an unbroken silence that was slowly but surely enveloping me. I stopped moving my arms, gave up resisting. And then, absolute peace. I was drowning in silence. It was all over. The Mondays, the Tuesdays, the Wednesdays, the Thursdays, the Fridays and Saturdays. The dirt and the cleanliness. Reality and unreality.

I don't even know what happened. Nothing, probably. I let myself go. As light as a feather, I let myself go. But then my legs started to move. My arms and feet started to fight back against the water. I started to kick my legs furiously with just one thought in my head:

No.

No.

No.

No.

I couldn't tell you where that impulse came from, what brought on that sudden feeling of determination. That's all that happened: those two letters. That was all I needed to haul myself like a fishing hook being dragged to the water's surface.

My head emerged, I took hold of the side of the pool, rested my forearms on the pebble tiles and breathed in all the air in the city, all the air on the planet. Next I started coughing and coughing. It took me a while to pull myself out of the water, and then I lay down face up by the edge of the pool. My eyes, wide open in a state of confusion, started to blink. A tiuque was circling the house with its wings spread wide. A few pale clouds were floating above the branches of the trees. And under the clouds and the branches, under the flight path of that scavenger, was I, alive.

I took several deep breaths until my heart stopped pounding. Then I sat up, stretched my arm out across the water and pulled on the girl's dress sleeve to drag her over to the edge. She wasn't easy to move. The ribbon waistband had got caught in the swimming pool filter. I had to really yank on it to pull it free, and it remained there, that pink sash, floating on the water like an omen.

I lifted her body out as far as I could, then pulled her by one arm before laying her out on the ground. My first thought was to close her eyelids. I also arranged her dress over her knees and placed her arms down by her sides. She looked beautiful in that white dress she'd so detested. Beautiful with her eyelids closed, her mouth closed, and her life, too, having come to a close.

I sat watching her for a long time, as if waiting for her to wake up. She would never wake again, and her memories would disappear with her, as would I, because I was just another one of those memories. I don't know what I felt. It's not relevant. I do remember asking myself if I would miss her songs, her races along the hallway, her permanent state of exasperation. And the answer was yes, of course I would miss her. And also no, not in the slightest.

I stood up and looked at the house from the back garden. That real house with its real terrace and its real bedrooms and bathrooms. Only then did I remember them: the señora, the señor. I wondered how the tragedy would spread across that man's face; how the news would engrave itself into the woman's devastated expression.

I walked across the garden dripping wet and entered the house through the dining room. Every step I took on the rug and parquet left dark damp halos that were no longer mine to clean. When I reached their bedroom door I hesitated, but not for long, and then I went in without knocking.

The señora was asleep on her back, her dental guard stained with blood. The señor was gently snoring, curled up like a child. I don't know how long I stood there watching them. A puddle was beginning to form at my feet when I felt a shiver and the alarm clock made me jump. It was seven o'clock in the morning. Their day was about to begin.

The señora fumbled around on her nightstand and turned off the alarm clock. She sat up and rubbed her eyes. It was as if she didn't trust them. Her eyes, I mean, and that's why she rubbed them until I appeared unmistakeably before her.

What's happened? she said.

The actual phrase she used was longer, but I couldn't make it out. Her voice woke the señor. He sat bolt upright. He already knew what had happened somehow, of course he did. He stared at the woman standing at the foot of his bed, gulped and spoke:

Julia, he said, getting to his feet.

Neither of them dared make another move. Nobody said anything. For the first time in all those years they gave me time to find the right words. And I stood there very still, as if that day contained millions of hours and I had at my disposal a limitless window in which to speak.

During my silent period I often wondered what my first words would be. If they would name something new or beautiful. Or if, perhaps, I would never speak again, and that new or beautiful thing would remain inside of me, safe from harm. The strange thing is that the words almost slid out of my mouth. My voice came out effortlessly. A little hoarse from so much silence, but clear enough to speak the truth.

The girl's dead, I said.

And the words even made a sound as they came out.

I couldn't bring myself to wait for their response.

I went out of the room into the hallway, then from the hallway to the front garden, which I crossed before finally opening the gate and leaving that house.

At first I walked slowly and hesitantly along the pavement, as if I didn't know where I was going. After a while my feet planted themselves more firmly until I could no longer stop.

I turned onto the main road and crossed over at the petrol station. On seeing me Carlos raised one hand and smiled. Then he noticed my soaking wet clothes and hair and his hand froze like that in the air, as if he could no longer move it. It seemed to me that he hesitated before speaking, that he couldn't find the words.

Are you okay? he said.

He took my hands but I pulled them away. His were warm and their warmth only made me notice how cold mine were. I could feel my sodden clothes, my hair dripping a wet course down my back, my feet damp inside these battered old plimsolls. He had a right to know, that's what I thought as I looked at him. He had loved that dog too, even if he did call her by another name.

Yany's dead, I said.

The day was growing hotter. A dry, stifling heat from which there was no escape. I cleared my throat and spoke again.

My mama's dead too. And the girl …

I stopped. The trio was complete.

Carlos wanted to know what had happened. I didn't reply. What did the cause matter? The streets were steadily filling with traffic. A line of cars was forming at the entrance to the petrol station.

I'm heading back south, I said suddenly.

I liked the sound of my voice. Or maybe I liked those words, which I should have spoken much sooner.

He was still confused, Carlos, staring intently into my eyes. I wondered if there, inside my eyes, he could already glimpse the land, the apple trees, the curlews, the clouds bursting over the sea.

A driver beeped his horn to get Carlos to come and serve him. He wanted the petrol attendant to fill his tank, clean his windscreen, check his air and oil. All for a tip. Carlos waved away the cars waiting in line.

He was breathing heavily, filling his chest with air. He was alive, is what I thought, and that thought made me happy. Carlos spoke again and this time his voice was firmer.

Let's head into the centre, he said. Now, let's go.

I didn't understand what he was talking about. The centre of what? Where? But nor did I ask. There was nothing more to say. I was going to leave that city once and for all.

I walked back to the pavement and began to pace down the street. You probably already know this, but Carlos followed me. At no point did I turn around. I've told you I didn't want to look back, but he walked behind me like a shadow. I didn't stop him, but I didn't speak to him either. I just wanted to get away from that house as fast as I could. To get away from the servant's room and the dead girl.

I wanted to forget them; do you understand? Rip them from my mind. But no matter how fast I walked, they were still there: the señor with his white coat and the white cuffs of his shirts; the señora in front of the mirror covering up her first wrinkles; and the girl, that furious child who had learned early how to walk, how to talk and how to order her maid about. The girl with her eyes open, her body drowned in the swimming pool. The girl I never should have loved and whom I loved all the same. That's people for you, I thought, and I could hear my mama's voice. That's what people are like, I kept repeating to myself, and those words spurred me on.

I could see the bypass one street away. I've already mentioned that there were never any buses in that neighbourhood, and that day was no exception. If the only way to get to the bus station was by foot, then so be it. I don't know how long I walked for. The rushing cars droned in my ears, the sun rose higher up my back and the emergency lane was narrow and dangerous, but none of that stopped me. Carlos didn't try to, either. Ask him, he was right behind me. I just kept looking ahead, prepared to walk all the way back to the open countryside if I had to, to swim across the canal. I need to get out, to leave this yellow-brown city where I never should have come.

I'd been walking for a long time when the bypass dipped underground. Everything went dark and out of focus and the roar was deafening. I was a few steps into the tunnel when a truck honked its horn at me. Startled, I stopped. My clothes and shoes felt heavy. There was no air down there. Only noise, darkness, oil stains on the tarmac. The cars kept zooming past, one after the other. They honked incessantly. And at that point I did have my doubts, I do remember this well. I couldn't be sure, write this down, if I was really there. Whether I was still in this world or it had continued on its course without me. I must have been run over, or worse: I must have saved the girl, dragged her to the edge of the pool, and now my body was lying in the water, face down in a maid's uniform, and the proof of my death was where I was standing in that tunnel: too far from the entrance and too far from the exit.

But it was there, the exit, that's what I told myself. The mouth of the tunnel growing steadily bigger, closer, brighter. I kept walking along the emergency lane, wondering as I went what must have happened after I'd left. If the señor or señora had called the police. Or whether, on seeing their daughter's body, they'd taken a load of pills: him, her, all the pills left lying around that house. Or if, maybe, when

I'd walked out, they'd gone looking for those bullets on the lawn and the señora had taken the handgun and shot a bullet through each of their hearts. The father and mother, the husband and wife, the señor and señora, finally silent.

Outside, the sunlight blinded me. It took a while to adjust to it, but reality gradually came back into focus. I noticed there were no longer any big houses around. The parks and wide pavements had gone too. Dirt, that's what I saw. Dust, that's what I felt. And people, more people than I had ever seen. They were tumbling out of shops, subway stations, buildings and offices.

It didn't seem strange to me at first. What did I know? I'd walked too far, worked too hard. I just wanted to get to the station as quickly as possible, so I took a path that ran alongside what used to be the river. The heat was wringing out the brows of the people around me, including Carlos, who appeared suddenly on that gravelly path, sweaty and red from the heat.

You nearly got yourself killed, he said, coming to walk at my side.

Immediately next to him was another woman, then another, then a man. So many people, that's what I thought. Each with their own jobs, their own work schedules, their own bosses. They all seemed to be going to the same place. I only noticed then that they were all moving in the same direction.

I walked alongside Carlos until we reached La Alameda, when it finally dawned on me what was going on. There were thousands of people there, you must already know that. Thousands of men and women already there, and thousands more arriving, filling the avenue. I realised I could no longer feel my feet moving. I could no longer hear my own voice. They blended in with the other footsteps, with the thousands of other voices. There were so many people that all the houses and buildings must have been empty. Apart from that one house. That house with the television tuned in to the news.

We shuffled along with the other bodies until we could go no further. I stopped and Carlos stopped too. I remember so clearly the look he gave me. Open, serene. That was the way a person should look at another.

He took me by the arm to keep us inching forward together. I didn't want to keep moving. My legs and feet ached. But all the same I advanced with those thousands of bodies. My eyes started stinging. Something was making my eyelids itch and preventing me from seeing ahead. I rubbed my eyes, now burning. The skin on my face was burning too. It must have been exhaustion, that's what I thought, and then I spotted the thick white cloud of gas slipping between my feet.

The air became hard, it stung, and between blinks I could barely glimpse what was happening just a few metres away. Trucks, uniforms, helmets, flashing police lights. This is the beginning of the part you know better than I do. One blast, then another. Insults, screaming. My eardrums felt like they were going to burst, my eyes were full of smoke. The gas was becoming gradually denser and pricking my eyes. Carlos shouted something I couldn't hear. It all happened so quickly. All around me people were running, trying to escape. I also wanted to escape, but my legs were paralysed with fear. I couldn't breathe. I stood there unmoving, surrounded by screams and shouting. The ones in uniform started charging. I would be next. My heart was pounding in my chest. That was the only sound: the beating of my heart. And then, out of nowhere, a vision. This isn't a digression, believe me. This is exactly what I saw: my mama drinking a mug of tea and looking at me from behind her fogged-up glasses, and Yany lying at her feet, also looking at me, and the girl next to her, stroking her head. There was no sense in being afraid. Afraid of what. Of losing what.

I took off running through the crowd and I could see Carlos was still beside me. He grabbed my hand and tried to pull me in his direction. Others were screaming, running away, crouching behind cars. They'd shut off the street, you could hear gunshots and the smell of smoke was all around. Through flames I spotted a feral dog growling at a group of policemen. One of them approached the animal and kicked it in the head. The dog fell silent and backed away in shock. I could feel my breathing become heavy and a burning sensation in my chest. Carlos gripped me with both arms, looked me squarely in the face and said one word:

Run.

He pointed towards a street corner. We splintered off into a smaller group, away from the throng. Swarms of men and women were running in all directions. We found ourselves up a side street where some boys were tearing up cobblestones from the ground. They would loosen them with crowbars, pick them up and then run to the front. Behind us, police. Ahead, more police. We're surrounded, I thought, looking down at the ground.

Under the stones the black earth was smooth, untrodden. I remember it feeling like a great discovery amid all the chaos: that black earth, and there, bent over it, defiant: Carlos. He grabbed a cobblestone, stood up and gave me that look. His eyes were watering from the tear gas, the black stain was there on his chest.

How much longer, he said, or that's what I think he said.

The noise became deafening, more gas was released. I lost sight of Carlos. I don't know if he threw the stone or not. It was swelteringly hot. All that fire, all that sun, all those bodies in the same space. I was so thirsty. How much time had gone by. How many breakfasts, how many lunches. How much cleaning, how much dirt. I felt my fingers twitch. I clenched and unclenched my fists, bent down and I too picked up one of those stones. That's right, I admit it, I took a rock in my hand.

A strange feeling came over me then, and I want to put it on record. A wound opened up in my gut, right here, and the pain forced me to stop. I realised that there was no way out. I couldn't reach the station. I wouldn't be going home to the south. Another minute longer and I would vanish from that street. It was as if I were in flames, you see? As if

I, too, were on fire. This was the last thing I could demand of my heart; the last thing I would ask of my legs.

With my hand raised above my head, I took off and ran. I ran like I'd never run before. The hand that I'd used so often to cook and clean and darn and iron – like the hand that you'll use to point and judge – held that rock firmly in its grasp. But at the same time, it was no longer mine. It was my mama's gnarled hand collecting stones on the beach, braiding another little girl's hair, cleaning the bathroom, mopping the floor, just as my hands had cleaned the bathroom and mopped the floor. And now, cupped in our hand was that stone, which we – which I – would pitch into the air with unnerving force.

Then I stopped and looked up. Above me, beneath the sun, that rock flew through the sky with hundreds of others. I didn't hear it fall. There was no way of telling that sound apart from all the others. Exhausted, I stood on the spot, unsure where to turn. The last thing I saw was the mountains. The sky ablaze. Then I felt something hit me on the back of the head, and after that, nothing, absolutely nothing.

I woke up in this place. In this very room I opened my eyes. I have no memory of getting here. I don't know how long I was asleep. I must have dreamed the slow descent down those steps, floor after floor, into an ever-greater darkness. I suppose I also dreamed the hazy vision of the land, my mama and me ploughing the earth, her hands and mine in that mud, until she told me she had to go because there was something urgent I needed to finish.

The pain at the back of my neck, right here, pulled me out of that dream. I think that's when I asked you for some water, you must remember that. And while I waited, impatient and desperately thirsty, I looked around at these peeled walls, at the door locked from the outside, at the mirror you're all hiding behind, and I had this thought: no one can withstand confinement like I can.

I've no idea how she drowned, whether the sash getting caught prevented her from swimming back up. Maybe, like the fig tree, she died from the sheer anticipation of the torturous future that awaited her. It's no longer important. I don't want to talk about her death anymore. You can forget what you don't name, and I'm done putting a name to it all.

I've finished, do you understand? This is my ending. I told you I wouldn't lie to you, and I've kept my side of the bargain. Now it's time for you to keep yours and let me out.

I need to go back to the south, even if that means returning to an empty house. I need to go and repair the floor and the roof and replant the vegetable garden. Pick maquis and apples, blackberries and currants. And sleep when I want to sleep. And eat when I want to eat. And at night, lying on my bed, hear the patter of the rain. A long, heavy downpour that soothes me through to dawn.

Now I'll ask you kindly to get out of your seats. Yes, I'm addressing you one last time.

Get up, find the key and open this door.

It's an order, that's right. An order from the maid.

I've finished speaking now. I've come to the end of my story. From now on you can no longer say that you didn't know. That you didn't hear or see. That you were oblivious to the truth, to reality.

I'm in here. The door's still locked.

I can't hear you over on the other side. I need you to open the door.

Hello?

Can you hear me?

Is anybody there?